To Mark [illegible]
God Bless [illegible]
Support our Troops
Randy Juge

TO NAM & BACK

Don't pray for me

Randy Juge

Llumina Press

ISBN: 1-59526-315-2
1-59526-316-0
Printed in the United States of America by Llumina Press

Library of Congress Control Number: 2004091866

In memory of Bob Hope (Leslie Townes Hope)
May 29, 1903 -- July 27, 2003.

Bob was considered by all to be an honorary veteran of all wars since World War II. He brought a piece of America to the GI in the foxhole. He will be missed.

CONTENTS

Acknowledgements 1

Prelude 3

Introduction 7

Chapter 1
My Heritage 9

Chapter 2
Flight training-Phase 1 & Phase II 17

Chapter 3
Hello, Vietnam 27

Chapter 4
My first day as Aircraft Commander 33

Chapter 5
Burnout and bad news 41

Chapter 6
My buddy, Fred 45

Chapter 7
My Purple Heart 51

Chapter 8
My best day in Nam 55

Chapter 9
Magnet-ass 63

Chapter 10
Extra duties 69

Chapter 11
Crew chief and door gunner 73

Chapter 12
Special assignments 77

Chapter 13
Incoming mortars 81

Chapter 14
Going home 83

Chapter 15
My return to Fort Wolters 87

Chapter 16
Good wars versus bad wars 93

Chapter 17
What it all means 95

ACKNOWLEDGEMENTS

My family is number one in my life and without their support I would have never attempted to write. Luckily, everyone in my family has a sense of humor and accepts me for all that I am.

I want to thank my wife, Anzia, who refused to read the book until it was finished. Now that's motivation. But without her love and support over the years; my life would have been incomplete. We are soulmates.

Thank you Mom, for your prayers, they may not have been in vain. If you had a computer and fewer kids, you could have written volumes. You are truly a super-mom and the smartest person I know.

PRELUDE

WHY ME?

Like so many veterans of past wars, there are times I reflect on why I was a survivor. The old saying, that "The bullet didn't have your name on it" seems to fit; but the saying, "Being in the wrong place at the wrong time," is the one that especially applies to helicopter pilots since they are moving targets. A little more or less air-speed can ruin your day!

I had thirteen aircraft shot up, and the only time I was wounded was when I was on the ground taking off out of a hot LZ (landing zone). Most of the time, Charlie (Viet Cong) was shooting up my tail boom and rotor blades. Considering Charlie was trying to hit the cockpit, it would appear that he didn't know how to properly lead an aircraft.

Looking back over the years after the war, I am grateful that I made it. I am glad to have experienced the pains and pleasures of life from birth to bills. It is wonderful to be alive! I try not to become obsessed with past events but look to the future--hoping to grow old gracefully and watch my grandchildren develop. But the ongoing question is still hanging out there: Why me?

GOOD LUCK/BAD LUCK

I have seen this phenomenon called luck, both good and bad, on both sides of the battle line. I remember the time we were flying over the Tay Ninh Plantation at 2,000 feet above the ground and Colonel Johnston in the rear seat saw two enemy armed soldiers walking down a path between the rubber trees. He called to the door gunner onboard to start firing at them as he fired his .45 cal (caliber) pistol with some tracer rounds so the door gunner would know where to shoot. The colonel actually hit and killed one of the enemy soldiers with that puny weapon. That was one unlucky bastard!

On the other hand, Charlie could be very lucky, like the time we were flying over Hobo Woods and we spied an enemy soldier at the bottom of a B-52 bomb crater. He was probably bathing in the pool of water at the bottom. We came down to about 800 feet and commenced firing. My left door gunner peppered the earth all around the poor bastard as he tried to climb out of the slippery crater. He fired until his gun jammed; so I circled in the opposite direction to let my right door gunner have at it. The bullets were all around Charlie but occasionally he would turn to fire his pistol at us. We eventually descended low enough to be almost "eyeball to eyeball" with him when my right door gunner's gun jammed. Charlie and I looked at each other as I saluted him and I pulled pitch (power) and left the area. What effect did I have on his life? Did he make it? Is he asking the same questions that I ponder? Did he have to retake that bath?

I look back with some amusement on the night that my copilot and I were sleeping in our hooch (living quarters) at Dau Tieng. I awoke with a startle at what I thought was a gun being fired in the hooch. I rolled out of my cot and grabbed my .45 cal and was looking for an enemy intruder. My buddy was on the floor, gasping for air and holding his chest. I crawled over to him, thinking the worst. Just as I reached him, I saw a huge piece of metal next to him. I looked up at the tin roof with its gaping hole letting the moonlight shine through. Lord, I thought, this could be nasty! I carefully rolled him over, expecting to see blood and guts. I saw nothing. He finally began to speak; I felt relieved

It turned out he was hit by friendly-fire when a 105-cannon shell prematurely exploded as it was fired over our hooch. Fortunately, it came through the roof flat side down and did not tumble like it would have if it had hit the 2 x 4 rafters. My buddy was not seriously hurt, and he tried, in vain, for months to get a Purple Heart. He didn't qualify because the incident was from "friendly" fire.

DON'T PRAY FOR ME

My family and wife were constantly inferring in their letters that they were praying for me and that they knew I would make it. After awhile it became a sore point with me; I actually wrote my mother and told her to stop praying for me. I told her that I would hate to think that other soldiers, who didn't have such a support group, would die. I felt that we should all be on the same-level playing field.

I was also concerned that if something did happen to me, my folks would live with guilt, thinking they hadn't prayed enough. My dad said to me before I left for Nam: "I can accept your death in combat doing your job, but don't get killed doing something stupid." I guess we all did at least one dumb thing in a moment of boredom; but for the most part I was not a cowboy (a reckless pilot).

LETTER TO MOM

0200 hours

I know that this will be kind of a touchy subject with you all but I must express my feelings. I believe in having a fate. I believe that God has little or nothing to do with it. That what we become is up to us, otherwise I could not take pride in my conquests and would have to blame Him for my failures. The guy who gets killed over here is not the one who has the fewest candles burning in a church or fewest prayers said by his loved ones. Prayers are said to praise God, not to ask for favors. Pray for forgiveness, for someone's soul, or for peace but not for favors.

A lot of good guys have died here and I am sure some of them may deserve dying. When I pray, and it's not a formal prayer, I ask only that he will give me strength to use my acquired skills to perform the mission successfully, and of course, just praying alone gives me courage.

I realize that your prayers probably give you faith and hope. They are doing some good since you believe this and worry less. If I came home and believed that they (your prayers) really saved me from death; I would feel guilty about my comrades who did die. That I upset the scale of life and death, no I must make it on my own. Let what be—be.

Your loving son
Randy

SPEAKING OF STUPID

Normally, the first mission of the day was to deliver hot food and plastic bags of water to troops on patrol in the jungle, and then fly low level down the muddy roadways to look for dung piles (booby traps) and mined bridges. On one such mission, flying from Tay Ninh to Dau Tieng, I flew over a convoy on the move with minesweeper personnel leading the way.

Shortly after I passed over them, I flew over a small bridge and noticed a shinny wire leading from the bridge out along the creek into some adjacent woods. Immediately, I turned the aircraft around and landed in front of the convoy, informing them of what was ahead. I returned to the bridge, flying low and slow, seeking the wires source. After a few minutes there was a tremendous explosion behind us. Looking back I saw a human form falling from a height of about 20 feet onto what use to be a bridge. I continued to follow the wire, hoping to fine the VC (Viet Cong) who had set off the explosives–but to no avail.

When I returned to the convoy, I found out that it was the major and his sergeant major that were killed trying to defuse the bomb. What in hell were they thinking?

Then there was the sad time a young lieutenant led his men across an open rice field in a charge against a .50-cal machine-gun emplacement. He got everyone in his platoon killed. The lone survivor was their dog. That was not bravery; it was stupidity. He should have called in an air strike.

This was a war of young men—impulsive and some times stupid. In past wars, there was a higher ratio of older men that provided guidance. I went to Nam at twenty-four; I was considered one of the old guys. In the early years of the war there were more “older soldiers” because a lot of career soldiers volunteered to serve in Nam to further their careers.

INTRODUCTION

I am a firm believer that everybody has a story. As a kid I always enjoyed listening to old people tell their stories. I guess it's time to tell mine. All Vietnam pilots are reluctant to tell their stories, except perhaps to other pilots who can appreciate the circumstances we all experienced. I was prompted to write my story after reading another book, ANGEL'S WING, by one of our pilots, Joseph R. Finch. Joe's book provides a good look at our unit as a whole; however, he only touched upon the everyday experience of a "slick pilot" in Nam. I wanted to give a little different perspective by presenting some of my observations.

Also, I became a little aggravated during a conversation I had with one of my present clients. He suggested that, because I was laid back and soft-spoken, I suffered from "Vietnam Syndrome." He said that he could get me 100 percent disability from the service. He didn't have a clue as to who we were and why we did what we did. It was not for financial compensation. I believe I was making (flight pay and hazardous duty pay) about $460 per month (not including room and board), which was half of what I made as a civilian. I laughed and said that he was barking up the wrong tree.

He said, "Well, then answer a few questions." I agreed. He asked if I go to see war movies. I replied, "Sure, some of them." His response was, "Well, it must be out of curiosity." He then asked when I go out to eat, if I always sit with my back to the wall. I laughed again and replied, "Not necessarily." He asked if I were divorced and I said, "Yes." He replied in a voice of triumph, "You have all the signs of Vietnam Syndrome." I really laughed as I said, "Mac, you have it all wrong. I joined the Army to get away from my ex-wife!"

Pilots were hand selected because of their physical and mental aptitude and also because they were problem-solvers and "Type A" personalities (motivated, confident and risk takers). Every pilot believes he is the smoothest, coolest and bravest aviator in the sky. All pilots were in Nam performing their mission not only for love of country, Mama and apple pie, but because they loved to fly and wanted to help the troops in the field. Woulda', coulda', shoulda' is not our way of remembering past events. All of the pilots I have spoken with are satisfied with their efforts in the war and have no regrets except the outcome.

In telling my story I am representing every slick pilot (as opposed to a gunship pilot) in my area of operation (III Corps). My missions represented the typical missions that every pilot in our unit flew. We all had opportunities to fly every mission assigned to our unit--from combat-formation flying, counter-mortar, defoliation, command and control (C&C), medevac (medical evacuation) and snifter missions--to courier and special assignments. It is not my nature to brag about my missions in Nam; so I apologize in advance if my story comes across that way.

CHAPTER 1

MY HERITAGE

I was born in New Orleans and grew up in what was then rural Metairie, Louisiana.

My mother (Florence) was an educator and my father (Frank) was an electrician. There was harmony in this relationship--a balance of Mom's intelligence and Dad's diligence. Mom motivated us to do our best and Dad taught us discipline and hard work by example. Their guidance produced a professor of chemistry (Frank), a nurse (Suzanne), a lawyer (Denis) and an insurance agent (me).

Mother was born in Hanoi, French Indo-China. Her father, a Swiss tobacco buyer, was a world traveler. Her mother died when she was three and she was raised by a succession of women whom her father befriended. She came to the United States when she was fifteen and by eighteen she had a college degree. Although her father came to America, he never became a naturalized citizen. He moved about the states creating business ranging from furniture repair to hand-rolled cigar shops. Quite an entrepreneur! He was also an international swordsman, respected for his ability with the epee.

My father's family line went back to the early 1800's. They first arrived from France and settled in Donaldsonville, Louisiana, up river from New Orleans. One of my great uncles, General Paul Juge, surrendered the city of New Orleans to Admiral Farragut during the Civil War. He eventually had to return to France since the citizens of New Orleans criticized him for keeping the peace during the Yankee occupation of the city. My grandfather (Alcee) was a Rough Rider at eighteen, and created a family business by introducing the first industrial scale from France. He opened a chemical laboratory and started a business of providing quality control between the seller and buyer of grains and cooking oils.

BEFORE I JOINED THE MILITARY

Looking back it seems that all my prior experiences prepared me for my role as a helicopter pilot. I was always an adventurer spending most of my childhood in the woods with my dogs. Later, I transferred this adventurous spirit into sports and held several records in track, and was voted most athletic by my senior class. After high school I accepted an athletic scholarship to Texas A&M University in track. Up to that point everything had come to me easy: school, sports, and life in general. However, shortly after entering college, I suddenly found that I actually had to study, and the level of competition in sports had taken a quantum leap from what I had previously experienced.

Even though I jumped over 6 foot 5 inches, it was not good enough to get fifth place at that level of competition. I gained too much weight to high jump, and my excellent form in the discus throw alone was not up to par with the physical strength of my competitors. My teammate, Randy Matson, could throw farther standing still than I could with a full spinout. So I accepted the head coach's suggestion to transfer my scholarship to football.

Unfortunately, the next year, Jean Stallions became the new football head coach and he was upset about my getting married during the semester break. He decided not give me the benefits of a full-marriage scholarship—thus denying me room and board off campus. I lived in married student housing jokingly referred to as "sperm village." My new wife had to get a job to help support us, and our money was real tight. Plus I had the added physical stress of intensive workouts, four hours a day, and seven days a week. They called it PE 107, and the team was later penalized for it.

My grades suffered to the point that I realized that I would never be able to get into the School of Veterinarian Medicine. I lost all incentive to continue so I quit. That last day on the practice field was pathetic. I could hardly perform a pushup. Coach John Pardie, the famous NFL running back and then our lineman coach, sympathetically asked, "What going on, Juge?" I told him that my desire to play football was gone and I intended to quit that day. He said, "I understand. Just lie back".

Coach Pardie arranged a meeting with the head coach after practice. Coach Stallions called me into his office and told me that if I quit, I would be a quitter the rest of my life. If nothing else, that statement motivated me not to fail again. Later that week I entered and won my first fencing tournament, defeating twenty-six more experienced competitors, and becoming the Southwest Champion with the epee. My fencing coach said he was impressed with my aggressiveness with my flashing blade.

That following summer I moved back to New Orleans and worked for a company that supplied chemicals to the oil fields. I worked with a maintenance crew traveling from dock to dock all along south Louisiana. Our jobs included sand blasting, welding and painting storage tanks, and loading ramps on the docks. The work meant spending each week away from my wife, adding more problems to our troubled marriage.

One lesson I learned while building bulkheads on the dock was that creosote (a toxic tar-base preservative used to treat pilings) would burn whatever skin is exposed to its fumes within three feet radius. No one in the crew was kind enough to inform this college boy about the caustic effects. And they thought it was really funny that I had to sleep in the trailer that night with my arms held up to the window air-condition to relieve the pain of the second degree burns on my arms and neck.

These guys also didn't point out the dangers of the welder's arc when I first started working with them. But thanks to a story my dad told me when I was a young boy; I realized that you do not look at a welding arc, even from a good distance, without burning the retinas of your eyes. My dad said one time he had a new helper and assumed he knew about the arc. Dad would say, "Watch the arc," just prior to striking the welding rod to the positive metal bar, but he was using common slang. It actually meant for everyone in the area to watch out for the burning arc, not look at it. Dad said that after a while the helper said, "Please, Mr. Juge, I can't watch that arc no more 'cause it burns my eye something fierce." Dad felt really bad. Don't assume!

On my last day at that job there was an incident that taught me not to assume anything. The whole summer, one of my coworkers (a pure Cajun, coonass) was constantly kidding me and playing pranks on me. I assumed that he had a good sense of humor and that we were friends. On my last day of work, he was full of his mischief. Jokingly, I picked his ass up over my head and walked down to the pier and threw him into the bayou. He came up gasping for air and I soon realized that he could not swim. I jumped in and pulled him out. If he had not panicked, he would have realized that the water was very shallow and he could have just stood up. The minute he hit dry land, he flew into a crazy fit trying his best to kill me! Others crewmembers kept us apart. I was just grateful that it was my last day on the job.

My prior experiences at welding and reading blueprints qualified me for my next position as a lab technician for Chrysler Space Division. The job encompassed setting up the platforms for testing and then actually testing the major components of the Saturn II rockets.

After my separation from my ex-wife I was a bit mean spirited about women in general and somewhat of a cad. Maybe a rascal is a better description. Within the plant there was an office made mostly of glass where the secretarial pool worked. The guys who worked in the plant had to pass by the "glass harem" on the way to the snack bar. Eventually I met Miss Pat--a good-looking, long legged, Cajun brunette who was very naïve.

I had grown a beard at this point in my life and wore the white NASA lab coat. My cousin Ricky Sigg who had just been hired was now working with me. When we were kids my mother always tried to keep us apart because she knew that when Ricky and I were together we would always find trouble.

I introduced Ricky to Miss Pat at the snack bar and she made a comment about nepotism. Ricky jokingly said, "Have you met Randy's twin brother Ronny yet?" I looked at him as he gave me a wink and I decided I would play along with him. The next day I shaved off my beard. Later that day when I walked past the glass harem, sure enough, Miss Pat came out and said, "You look younger without your beard." I said, "Oh, you have me confused with my brother, Randy." "I'm Ronny." She took the bait. The next day I took off the lab coat. When she approached, she had a puzzled look on her face as though she were afraid to call out my name. I said, "I'm Randy. My brother said that you didn't like the beard so I shaved it off." It was embarrassing to see her stutter.

Ricky and I fooled her for over a month. I even dated her twice, as each of the two personalities. The truth came out after Miss Pat's supervisor had spoken to my supervisor. Apparently Miss Pat was getting upset and her frustration was affecting her work. My cousin and I broke the news to her and she actually forgave us. However, I could not get a date with any girl in the glass harem after we played that practical joke.

All my coworkers were prior military members and had learned their skills while in the service. They influenced my thinking about the value of military service. Up to that point I had never thought too much about serving in the military.

Although I did not avoid the draft, fate had the draft avoided me until I volunteered. When I was at Texas A&M, all college men were exempt. By the time I left college, I happened to be married and married men were also exempt. Later, with a divorce pending, I was exempt because I was working for Chrysler/NASA Space Division. However, when Chrysler started to announce some layoffs, an old Navy veteran with whom I worked, encouraged me to join the service. He also told me that it would be foolish not to apply for some military school and suggested that I apply for helicopter pilot training. I didn't even know how to spell helicopter pilot, but now "I are one." Sorry, bad joke.

JOINING THE ARMY

I always thought it was a tragedy that some young men avoided the draft by going to Canada. (If you knew how to type, you could avoid combat.) For every soldier in a combat environment, there were eight personnel behind the line of fire supporting him. For every man assigned to Nam, there were twenty men assigned to other parts of the world. The law of probability was in your favor; and the higher your scores, the lower the probability that you would end up on the front line.

My dad had taught me at an early age to work with my hands, so I had a good basic knowledge of tools. Working as a lab technician, I was well acquainted with blueprints and could visualize in the third dimension. This knowledge prepared me for the written flight-aptitude test I had to take, even though I had never flown an aircraft. And physically, I was in great shape. Even though there was a long waiting list to get into flight school, there was a cancellation and I was offered the spot if I could report for the service in three days. I jumped at the opportunity.

My older brother Frank drove me, early in the morning, to the old Custom House at the foot of Canal Street in New Orleans for my induction into the Army. After another physical I took the oath and boarded a military bus for Fort Polk, Louisiana. Typically, as we came off the bus, a drill instructor "DI" was screaming in our faces as he marched us to an old warehouse where we picked up our bedding and uniforms. They fed us and then locked us in a barracks for our first night. The whole time I was wondering, "What the hell have I done?"

It is amazing how the military can take someone off the street and mold him or her into a highly-disciplined person in such a short time. The process involves completely stripping a person of his individual personality and then rebuilding his attitude and confidence from the ground up. Yes, it is a form of brainwashing, but it is controlled and produces positive results. I witnessed the process firsthand. Whoever I thought I knew on the bus on our way to the army base--by the end of the next day I could not pick him out of a group of soldiers. We were all baldheaded. After a while I found that I could only recognize other soldiers by looking at their eyes; this is a habit I still practice today. Their soul is in their eyes.

After regimented orientation and more tests, we were herded like cattle to a remote corner of the base called the company area. To this day I have no idea where I was. We began basic training coping with all the horrors that basic training has been known for, over its history.

The drill sergeant made me a platoon leader probably because of my size, age and prior ROTC training. My first leadership position proved embarrassing as I divided the squads up by racial orientation. I had the old southern bias from my childhood but that was quickly eliminated by my close association with these fine young men. As the weeks passed, I developed tremendous respect for those men to have even put up with my bias. I learned a great deal about leadership, men, and how the misuse of rank can touch many lives in negative ways.

I had one soldier who was absent without leave (AWOL) from basic training. I had been in his face a lot that week. I realized that my actions could affect the lives of others. The soldier in question was immature and obviously not ready for the pressures of military discipline, and it was probably best that he was rift out of the service for the sake of his fellow troop's in future combat situations. But I was not as gung-ho after that incident and realized that rank has its responsibilities and that power should not be abused. I learned a valuable lesson--to motivate men one must lead with compassion and insight.

One of the benefits that military service has given to each generation is to expose them to a melting pot of different races and backgrounds, forcing them to work together and develop respect for each other. This is the type of bond that our society needs to encourage. It's amazing what the drill sergeants accomplished in eight weeks: making us soldiers.

The most memorable day in basic training was Easter morning when we boarded a cattle truck at 4 A.M. in pouring rain to go to chapel. We were all dressed in an OD rain-poncho and piss-pot. The church was full to the brim with wet soldiers. This would be the last service before each of us would depart Fort Polk, take a short leave, and then be shipped off to Nam or another school for advanced training. As I looked around the room, I envisioned this scene appearing on the cover of LOOK magazine. It was a picture of stark reality—like those illustrated by Norman Rockwell.

CHAPTER 2

FLIGHT TRAINING

FLIGHT TRAINING-PHASE I

All pilots, both warrant officers and commissioned officers, were trained (at least in their primary phase of helicopter flight training) at Fort Wolters in Mineral Wells, Texas. As a warrant officer candidate (WOC), I entered the program directly out of boot camp with the rank of E-5, at least for pay purposes. Some candidates had already attained a higher rank because of their prior service but we were all treated equally--like shit!

It was a great time in our lives: every day was a new adventure--learning how to fly in an accelerated course, plus the regimental atmosphere of a military cadet school. You know, the "Sir, No, sir" bit, spit and polish, and everyone scalped!

When we arrived at Fort Wolters, we were assigned for a week in a holding company allowing time to get our uniforms and supplies up to flight school standards. We were all chomping at the bit to get our colored flight baseball caps and be assigned to a flight class.

Our flight training encompassed four components: academic, physical, flight, and discipline. Most of the instructors in all four components were warrant officers who had returned from Nam. The TAC officer was a warrant officer who was assigned to keep us in line and shape us into officer material. We were his to harass in the company area. At first he did his level best to scare the hell out of us! There would always be a couple of guys in platoon formation whose appearance he didn't like. Even a smile could get a WOC a lot of yelling. And the TAC officer would get so close to your face you could smell his breath as he yelled. He loved to ask loaded questions for which there was never a correct answer.

My TAC was Mr. Eddie. After a while it became amusing to watch him in action just as long as I was not his next victim. I always wondered how I would have responded to his questions like: "Candidate are you beedy-eyeing me? "Of course your first response would be, "Sir, no sir." Wrong answer! He would then ask, "Why not? Is it because you don't like me?" Of course there was no correct answer to that question without getting into more trouble. One day he noticed a guy who had a slight morning shadow so he asked him if he were a fighter or a lover. The macho answer was, "fighter, lover, or both." He always had a comeback that left the WOC stuttering.

I arrived with no money and even had to hock my Playboy Club card for $30 to have enough money to pay for uniform alterations and supplies. We learned quickly to have items such as soap, toothpaste, shaving kit, etc., that were never used but neatly stored in our locker as a "static" display for daily inspections. We were allowed one small cabinet, which we could lock, in which to hide personal items we actually used. We found out later even the locker was not a sacred space. Everything that could be seen had to be perfect. If the TAC Officer found an item not up to his standards, he would trash the whole locker and room. We spent most of our free time either waxing the floor or staying off it so that we would not scuff it. I spent many hours perched on the windowsill reading.

Just when we thought we had everything perfect, Mr. Eddie discovered we were dumping our cigarette ashes down the bedpost tube. And then there was the time he found a dead fly on the windowsill. He declared the fly to be a fellow aviator and we were required to give it a military burial to include honor guards in dress-blue uniforms.

It was an amazing sight to see hundreds of helicopters flying out of the main heliport every morning, like bees leaving a hive. Our platoon in flight school was separated by height, so my squad was composed of the big guys 6'2" and taller. My roommate and student stick-buddy was big John Gennett who was 6'5". I was 6'4". Together we took up a lot of space and added a lot of weight to our trainer helicopter, the OH-23. When we flew together, I had a hard time pulling up on the collective control because John's huge ass overlapped the top of his collective control stick on his side that also moved my collective control stick in unison.

The comradeship of being a member of a group, challenged toward a common goal, formed a lifetime bond: or maybe it was just the bar fights we had together. My four buddies in those early months as WOCs were Big John, Pat Lawlor, Keith Galloway and Tom Landry. Big John learned to fight in the pool halls of Chicago. He showed no mercy when he entered a fight. I was surprised to see Pat with his big smile and blond hairs enjoy an occasional bar skirmish since he had the look of the all-American nice guy. Keith looked like Yul Brenner with his bony baldhead. He would always be ready on the sideline to help push you back into the pile if you were ejected from the fight. Tom had the look of a prizefighter and somehow would always be in the middle of the mayhem.

Bar fights were somewhat of a new experience for me since I was large enough that no one really messed with me. The few fights I had experienced growing up were more like wrestling. Besides, I never had the desire to smack anyone in the jaw.

I remember the time John and Pat challenged a couple of cowboys to a game of eight ball at a local pool hall, near the base. The bet was a dollar and John and Pat lost the first game. John tossed a dollar on the table and the other guys began to argue that the bet was a buck apiece. There was a push by someone and the next thing I knew, pool sticks were flying across the room and the opponents multiplied. I couldn't believe it when Big John deliberately stepped on some prescription eyeglasses that fell to the floor during the brawl. That dollar bet was getting expensive!

We won the fight but hoped that it would not be reported to the base commander. I didn't get into another fight until I was transferred to Fort Rucker, Alabama. By then it had become a weekend sport at the Oasis Club, off base with a new sidekick "Dog," John Stafflien, so named because he would say, "Woof," when he saw a pretty girl.

Not knowing if we would wash out of the flight program was always a reality that we had to deal with daily. The first hurdle was to hover and then to solo. There was a tremendous relief of pressure and privilege to be thrown into the Holiday Inn swimming pool--fully clothed—the day we soloed. Every once in awhile you would hear about a student's being killed on a solo flight and you didn't want to end up in that statistics entry. Sometimes you would hear about some WOC being washed out for taking a farmer flying, or some other stupid violation. It was always hard not to give in to the urge to test your limits as a new pilot. I admit now that I made some practice "red tire" landings reserved only for instructors, but the authorized "white tires" had become old hat.

There was one time that increased my pucker factor when I did a red-tire pinnacle landing on a cliff above the Brazos River. I didn't realize until after I landed that I was on an upward slope with my helicopter tail boom leaning down toward the river, and with the face of the cliff to my front about 20 feet high. Just like Arthur Riley in the 1950 sitcom THE LIFE OF RILEY, I mumbled to myself, "What a revolting development this is!" According to the training manuals, I was supposed to get out of the aircraft and measure the distance behind the aircraft to see if I would have enough running distance to successfully take off. Forget that idea--I had to keep maintaining power just to keep the helicopter from tumbling off the cliff backwards!

I realized I could not turn the aircraft around without causing mast-bumping, or even worse, having my tail rotor hit the upper slope. So, the only logical thing to do was to back up as far as I dare and try a forward take off, hoping that my trainer had enough power to climb over the cliff in front of me. All appeared to be going according to plan until I reached the top of the cliff: there stood a "dang" Texas tree growing at the top. Fortunately, my lift improved as I achieved true flight and I managed to fly over the tree. As I look back on the experience, I know the winds were kind to me that day. Knowing what I know now about down-drafts, I am thankful for the light winds that day.

One morning I saw Big John land in a riverbed to a white-tire; so I decided to join him. It was against the rules for two aircraft to land to the same tire at the same time. I landed 50 yards away from him. I got out and walked up to his aircraft to ask him for a lighter. He was deep in concentration, performing a textbook shut down. I tapped on his window and almost gave him a heart attack! I then realized that he hadn't heard me fly into his location.

I knew that I was a real helicopter pilot once I was into the program long enough to be eligible to purchase a MGB model sports car. The typical officer in flight training bought a Corvette to elevate his status above the WOC. The car salesman had a thriving business, with virtually no overhead. There were so many MGBs in the parking lot of our company area that I had to put an unusual bumper sticker on mine to help identify it. Of course, I would only have use of it for a few more months before I was sent to Nam; but Hey, what the hell!

FLIGHT TRAINING—PHASE II

I arrived at Fort Rucker, Alabama, the first week after New Year's 1968. After reporting to the WOC company headquarters, I walked over to my assigned billet. It was a typical old World War II, two-story, white barracks. It was winter and the smoke bellowed out of a brick chimney, filling the sky with a low ceiling of black smoke. As I walked into my room, my new roommate, Pete, pointed to a bed in the corner and said, "That one is yours." I vaguely remembered him from Fort Wolters as a member of another flight platoon. There was always a little animosity among the different flights, so it took a little while for us to accept our fate—we were stuck with each other as roomies.

Pete was the kind of guy with whom you had a love/hate relationship. He was wild and irresponsible but funny, and I was always covering for him. I had to make the beds, wax the floors, etc., with spit and polish for inspections. Pete would show up at the last minute, having been out all night. But his antics made you laugh. He was thin and had an olive complexion. His bone structure with his high cheekbones reminded me of an Indian warrior. He always seemed to have a lot of energy, and could talk his way into a nun's bed.

Pete had a reputation for driving over the Alabama speed limit signs with his old Buick, traveling at 80 miles per hour. The signs lay flat as a pancake along the sides of the Alabama highways as if he were staking out his territory. He was delighted to be assigned to gunship training. It amazed me that the Army picked the crazy guys to fly gunship. They must have picked them by their bad driving records!

As well as I knew him, I still made the mistake of loaning him my new MGB. He returned it the next morning, steering it with a crescent wrench. He claimed that someone had stolen my beautiful, leather-wrapped steering wheel. He told me the bad news while we were standing at attention in platoon formation so I couldn't kill him!

I had to forgive Pete for all the hell he gave me since he was the one who introduced me to my lovely wife, Anzia. The last week in flight school we had permission to live off base. Naturally, Pete jumped at the opportunity to live off base and to party more. We rented a unit in the old Daleville Inn just outside the main gate.

Pete was out carousing while I was lying on the couch--barefoot, shirtless, and relaxed. Someone knocked on the door. Half asleep I opened it to find Pete's girlfriend and her coworker, my Anzia. They were civilian nurses at the Army base and had been invited by Pete to come to his party. I knew nothing about any party; but when I saw this lovely creature at the door, I welcomed them both in and ran to put on a shirt and comb my hair.

My wife later said that she was not impressed at all with this barefoot boy who came to the door but I grew on her as the night unfolded. I tried to ignore the engagement ring on her left hand. I had been divorced earlier that year and was not really looking for love; but after seeing Anzia, I changed my mind. I began to strut like a barnyard rooster! The next day when she didn't show up with her friend at our next party, I went looking for her. I found her at her trailer and talked her into coming. She may have been having second thoughts about her fiancé. He was a first lieutenant in Nam; I pulled a "Jody" on him and won her over. Jody was the term applied to the civilians back home who were dating soldiers' girlfriends, resulting in the girlfriends mailing "Dear John" letters to Nam

I graduated from flight school April 9, 1968; I was now officially a "Mister Juge!" Immediately after the graduation, Anzia and I drove down to Panama City, Florida, for a fling in the surf for a couple of days. Then I had to get back to New Orleans to see my folks for a few weeks before I left for Nam. Soon after I got home I called Anzia to ask her to come down to New Orleans. She flew into town and we commenced where we left off in Panama City. Two days later we were on a ferryboat crossing the Mississippi River to the courthouse in Gretna, Louisiana, getting married before a judge. There happened to be another young couple at the courthouse getting married before the husband left for Army flight school. They stood in as witnesses at our wedding and we stood in as theirs.

That night we told our folks. I am sure they had their doubts about our whirlwind, 20-day courtship and five-day honeymoon before I boarded my flight to Nam. However, my relatives put together a crawfish-boil party so that everyone could welcome my new wife to the family. I took a 4 x 4-inch American flag from the party and glued it to the back of my flight helmet as a memento of our family get-together and for good luck.

My wife and I have been married for over 33 years and we have proven to everyone that love at first sight can last forever. Anzia is my soul mate. I admit that I did not marry her for her cooking, but I was pleasantly surprised at her maternal instincts and how well she reared our children. She blessed me with two wonderful kids, Allison and Clint, who in turn, gave us five terrific grandchildren: Little Randy, Jeb, Christopher, Clayton, and beautiful Ella.

Daughter Allison and Family

Love at first sight must run in our genes since our kids were as impulsive in love as their parents! Clint met Julia Hurd and a few months later they were married by the barber/justice of the peace in the small town of Madisonville. My daughter Allison met Chris Blossman at our family owned barbershop and they were engaged in a few months after their first date. Vive L'amour!

Son Clint and Family

Randy and Anzia

DEPARTURE TO NAM

The last days home were great but not ample to really get to know this new love in my life. It surely would have been a tragedy if I did not make it back from Nam. But like every good soldier, I boarded the plane and was off to a new experience that changed my life. A quick hop to Seattle, Washington, to spend the night at an Army base there, and then it was my last chance to call home before heading for Nam. With a stop in Anchorage, Alaska, and a short holdover in Japan, I got to see a lot of snow in Alaska and a mountain with snow on top in Japan. I guess I can always say that I have been there; adding to the small list of places I have visited, which up to that time was limited to five southern states.

When I finally arrived in Cameron Bay, Vietnam, I knew immediately that this place was definitely different from the five southern states. As I stepped off the plane onto the airstrip, the blast of heat on my face was a welcome change from being half frozen on our 13-hour flight. The airline pilot must have been from Alaska: he was still wearing his ski jacket. The first obvious thing I noticed was a lot of barbed wire and sandbags—everywhere. I mean everywhere! Staying there for one night was too long! That night at the officer's club I listened to all the war stories of the pilots who had finished their tour in

Nam and were returning home. If half the stories were true, my tour would not be a walk through the tulips. In any case it gave me more to think about.

I remember how indignant I became upon observing how the MPs treated the Vietnamese hooch maids as they entered and departed the base camp; but by the end of that week, I learned to be in complete agreement with the necessity for body searching as a security procedure. No matter how innocent their appearance might seem, you never knew for sure who were the bad guys or girls, and so you learned never to assume otherwise--for your own survival.

I spent the next few days doing what the Army calls the shuffle: fly north to the DMZ, landing at Da Nang; spend most of the day there; lift off in a C-130 cargo plane for a long flight south to Saigon; and stay at a holding company just outside Saigon at a place I now know as Red Carpet. After riding to Saigon International Airport every day for four days, I finally caught a flight on another C-130 to my final destination, Cu Chi, the birth place of Ho Chi Minh, the leader of the North Vietnamese forces.

CHAPTER 3

HELLO VIETNAM

On the first flight a pilot takes when he arrives at Saigon, his eyes automatically look to the northwest to see a lonely mountain standing out of place in the low plains of the Mekong Delta. Nui Ba Den (Black Virgin Mountain) is of volcanic origin--unlike the salt-dome hills that I am used to seeing in the marshes of Louisiana--like Avery Island. Nui Ba Den is bordered by the ancient city of Tay Ninh about five clicks (5,000 meters) to the west, and the Old French Fort, one click to the west. The Old French Fort was the last stand for the French when they occupied South Vietnam; there was a massacre of all the French troops defending the camp.

Hello Vietnam

French Fort North of Nui Ba Den

The mountain itself is famous for a U.S. massacre that happened during my first month in-country. The U.S. Army radio encampment perched on top of Nui Ba Den was overrun and twenty-three men were killed. The strange thing was that the commander of the camp was found dead with a 2 x 4 in his hand and all the weapons were locked up, untouched! Were those men so complacent about defense that they didn't even consider Charlie might attack them, high on the mountain?

The road at base of Nui Ba Den

It was commonly understood that we owned the top, with its radio camp, and the very bottom, where the Corps of Engineers had a rock-crusher plant built to supply material for building roads. However, Charlie owned everything in-between. In fact, it was rumored that Charlie had a network of tunnels inside the mountain to act as a rest and relaxation (R&R) center for their troops. Also, there was the possibility that the enemy even had a tunnel coming to the mountain from as far as the Cambodian border. Nah!

ARRIVAL AT THE 25TH INFANTRY DIVISION

When I arrived in Nam, I was initially assigned to the 25th Infantry Division, flying OH-23 models in support of an artillery unit. Soon after, I was offered a position with the Little Bears (Company A) as a slick pilot flying Huey models. I traded assignments with another pilot, Jim. I found out later that Jim was aware that the new LOH models, fully equipped with mini-guns, were going to replace the OH-23 model. If I had known, I probably would have stayed with the old unit. But ignorance can be a blessing; Jim was killed later that year, hovering above the trees, playing hunter-killer.

I didn't know Jim well, but he was a good pilot and great guy. I knew he had had a family problem earlier that year when his wife appeared in a Playboy magazine. He found out the hard way--by reading a copy. He flew home on emergency leave and came back about two weeks later. His mind may not have been in the cockpit on that fatal mission.

OUR MISSION

Every day in Nam you woke up to a reality check. From the first moment you awoke and looked around, you confirmed two things: Yes, I am still alive, and the bad news is that I am still in Nam. There were always moments during the day when you wondered what your family would be doing back home at that same time in space. Due to time-zone differences, we had to imagine them safe in bed. It was always interesting trying to imagine home, just as now I try to imagine Nui Ba Den; both exist at the same time but in different places. They do not disappear just because you are no longer there: obviously, life goes on.

A good example of a reality check was when we were involved in a battle south of Saigon. In addition to the wartime sounds of explosions and gunfire, there was the occasional sound of thunder from a 747 Pan American jet liner leaving Saigon Airport for the U.S.A. Every soldier in that firefight glanced up at the "Freedom Bird" and thought about the day when he would be taking that flight and looking down at Saigon, not up.

Pilots live by a code of honor to assist other pilots in trouble and aid our troops in the field. Like the knights of old, the helicopter pilots were the Templars of the Vietnam War. Their steed--the helicopter--wore the armor that was nothing more than a shell of aluminum-magnesium that had an affinity for fire and burned like a sparkler once ignited. But like the knight, we could ride into battle, strike the enemy, and ride out. The great thing about being a helicopter pilot was that you were normally exposed to enemy fire for ten minutes and then you were out of range. The poor grunt (infantryman) had to stay and endure the enemy fire until the battle was over.

I was glad to fly Hueys, the Cadillac of helicopters at that time. I was assigned to fly mostly command & control (C&C) missions. My first aircraft commander (AC) was Mr. Henry Henson who taught me, the copilot (shorten to just pilot in Nam) the "new rules" such as: avoiding the dead-man zone, making high overhead landings into hot landing zones (LZ), thinking ahead of the aircraft, never taking off into the wind if the enemy is on the windward side, and thinking of alternative solutions when things go amiss. As the pilot, I was responsible for monitoring radios, checking artillery crossfire, and learning the "new rules."

Our aircraft was outfitted with a lot of radios to provide the colonel with communication so his men could accomplish their mission. The primary mission I witnessed during 1968-69 was "search and destroy." Company-size fire support bases were established near an area suspected of housing Viet Cong. Daily patrols would be sent out each day looking for any evidence of enemy camps or ammo caches, and they would sometimes end up in a firefight. Charlie would intentionally wound the lead man when he was close enough to his (Viet Cong) position so we wouldn't be able to use air or artillery support without injuring our own man. Then our troops would spend the rest of the day trying to get the wounded man out—usually losing a few more soldiers in the process. The enemy knew how much we valued our men and he used that fact against us. I saw this scenario over and over again from my first to my last week in Nam. It was frustrating for me to watch; it was even harder on the ground troops who were trying to save a friend and comrade.

Except during the Tet offensives, Charlie would attack main bases and fire-support bases when we least expected it. Patrols might be ambushed during the day, but the major attacks were normally at night. Most of the battles were defensive battles: we normally kicked ass with all the fire support we had at our command. It was always an exciting mission to fly. There was even a sense of beauty watching all the .50-cal tracers coming up looking like bright snowballs in slow motion. I felt that I could dodge them with my aircraft like a bull-fighter--Ole! In between the snowballs was what we had to worry about.

Usually Charlie had anti-aircraft emplacements set up in a triangle formation to provide crossfire at the gunship rolling in on any one of their gun positions. To witness a Cobra- gunship following the line of tracers coming up at him and returning fire with rockets and mini-guns was impressive.

There was a lot of danger flying over a battlefield at night. You were constantly watching out for other aircraft that you had to assume were flying at a different attitude. Some of these were: helicopter gunship, C&C ship (flying the battalion commander), artillery observation ship, flare ship, jets and their flack-ship (fixed-wing aircraft firing spotter rockets), "spooky" (a C-130 equipped with mini-guns) and perhaps even a formation of combat assault helicopters circling wide for an approach. With artillery fire coming into the area from three different locations, we could only hope that we were not flying into the trajectory of a 105 shell. There were always smoke and low clouds to obscure our view. Things really got tense when Charlie fired his quad-50 and all the aircraft in the area turned off their beacon and navigation lights for a while. We were an accident waiting to happen, but somehow we managed not to collide with each other.

Charlie didn't like attacking on a full moon; so black is a good description of what you could see. On a clear night you might see a slight glimmer of lights from the Saigon airport. But most of Nam was dark with occasional pot fires from a village. On a moonlit night we saw reflections from the water in rice patties or bomb craters (of which there were plenty).

FLYING BLIND

Today's modern ground positioning satellites (GPS) would have been great to have but we had to fly strictly by time, airspeed, and compass direction. I used my aircraft direction finder (ADF) a lot. It looked like a compass with a big needle. I would get the unit to keep talking on their Fox Mike (FM radio); the direction-finder needle would home in on their position, pointing to the direction of their transmitter. If I flew past the transmitter, it would cause the needle to point to the rear of the aircraft

One time, I was flying as a copilot for another aircraft commander. We left a combat area to refuel and were flying back when the ground unit called and asked for a med-evac for a soldier with a sunken chest-wound. Because we were in the monsoon season it was raining heavily, and the aircraft commander told General Williams, in the rear seat, that he would have difficulty locating the troops in the rain. I asked why not use the ADF. He agreed with me and had the unit talk to us on their Fox Mike. We flew low-level right to them and landed just outside the ground action. The rain gave us cover from the enemy.

They put the injured lad in the cargo compartment with his entrails wrapped in a plastic bag to keep them from contaminating his body cavity, and used another plastic bag to cover a hole in his chest to prevent the air in his lungs from escaping. The aircraft commander and the general both received a Silver Star for saving the soldier's life.

I gained the respect of my aircraft commander who recommended me for promotion to AC because of my quick reaction to emergency conditions, and my flying ability. So, after only four weeks in country, I was given my own aircraft to command. Unfortunately, I was assigned to take over a C&C mission for a new battalion commander whom I shall now introduce as Colonel Chicken Shit.

CHAPTER 4

FIRST DAY AS AIRCRAFT COMMANDER

One of my first missions for Colonel Chicken Shit was to land inside the perimeter of a fire support base on top of the command bunker because the perimeter was heavily mined. He returned to the aircraft with his normal entourage--the sergeant major, his driver, and his executive officer (XO)--he also invited the company commander and his entourage to come for a ride. I told the colonel that I could not take off safely with all of them and the heavy console of radios. I mentioned that if I lost power, we would probably go down in the minefield. He took the hint and immediately agreed to leave with just the original crew.

It was the next fire-support base that provided the most amusement. I landed just outside the perimeter—the normal procedure to prevent the troops from eating my dust. Soon after the colonel and sergeant major jumped off the helicopter and were about 10 meters away, we started receiving incoming mortar rounds. Charlie was trying to bracket fire onto our position. I glared at the colonel to see if he intended to return to our aircraft. He appeared to be frozen. He was looking in the direction of the base camp looking indignant as though he wanted to give someone a court-martial for firing rounds near him.

Just then the sergeant major jumped on board and I immediately began to add power. I pulled up and to the left to avoid incoming mortar fire; my aircraft was tilted on a 45-degree angle. Just about that time the colonel decided to come aboard. He had one hand on the door and the other hand on the bottom of the door gunner chair, but his feet were in free space perpendicular to the ground as he hung out of my aircraft. The sergeant major grabbed him by his blouse (shirt), accidentally pulling off a big chunk of his chest hairs, and hauled the colonel's ass into the chopper. The colonel would have to stay away from the swimming pool for a while until he grew a new batch of chest hairs.

That was the colonel's first taste of combat in Nam. As I continued to fly to our base camp at Dau Tieng, he tapped me on the shoulder and requested that I climb to 2,500 feet altitude, and stay there for the return trip. Soon after, we were flying between thunderclouds, and a bolt of lighting passed between by skids. I looked over my right shoulder and came face-to-face with the colonel who was perched on top of the radio console behind me. That's when we nicknamed him Colonel Chicken Shit. With a straight face I said, "Welcome to Nam." The ground troops picked up on our nickname when the colonel imposed a moratorium on drinking beer at the fire support bases in the field. Ale rations have been a tradition which played a unique role in the history of warfare, as a perk for the soldier since before Romans times. The Roman soldiers were paid in salt but the ale was for their morale. It was a big mistake to mess with the troop's beer.

A SAD DAY

Colonel Chicken Shit worked at looking the part of a field combat officer. He would have us fly back to base camp by noon so that he could catch the midday sun. At first I thought the colonel had staff briefings, but later the sergeant major told us that the colonel would lie on a deck chair with a facial sun reflector to give him that bronzed look when he attended the generals' briefings in Saigon. It must have worked: I understand he made general. He was not a leader of men, and from what I saw; he was an asshole! I respected all the other colonels I flew; however, Colonel Chicken Shit was an idiot who cost the lives of twenty-five good men because of his incompetence as a military leader and his efforts for self-glory.

"Dumber than dumb" describes the events of November 24, 1968. The date sticks in my mind since it was Thanksgiving eve. It started out with usual morning missions--flying to one field base after another, ending up in Tay Ninh where we picked up a POW, and were flying back along Highway One toward Saigon. When we flew over the area east of Ben Cui, the prisoner was pointing out an area below. It was a large open area between two rubber tree fields with a wooded area on the north side bordered by a creek. Apparently that was his base camp. It was about 50 meters wide and 200 meters long and tapered at each end.

Rubber Plantation Thnaksgiving Day

The simple solution would be to call in air strikes to obliterate the entire area with napalm. But then the Air Force would get the glory! So we flew back to Dau Tieng and Colonel Chicken Shit called his staff to plan a ground assault using his tanks and armored personnel carriers. By noon, the convoy of tanks and troops were on the road planning to travel 20 miles over mine-filled roads. Several vehicles broke down en route; and sweeping for mines along the way caused them to arrive at the large open field about two hours before dusk.

The plan was doomed from the start but the colonel insisted on commencing the attack. The tanks and armored personnel carriers (APC) lined up along the length of the field; the line of vehicles moved toward the enemy line with ground troops behind them. They managed to get within 20 meters of the perimeter of the woods when the troops charged into the hedge line. Of course, the enemy started firing on the troops, and firing RPG (bazooka) at the tanks, hitting a couple of them. The tanks withdrew to the rear, leaving the troops pinned down in the hedge line.

The illustrious Colonel Chicken Shit then decided to personally drop a CS (tear gas) canister from our aircraft onto the enemy position, only to cause pain to our own men trapped in the hedge line. Darkness descended and we already had several men wounded or killed in the hedge line.

Next, the colonel ordered an airborne combat assault to land on the north side (the other side) of the creek. The landing zone was marsh, so the troops were up to their asses in mud as they jumped off the helicopters in the dark. To make things worse, as the troops advanced and fired into the hedge line, our troops on the other side were in their line of fire. Charlie was safe in his tunnels, popping out occasionally to fire at both north and south sides of his perimeter. About that time, Charlie fired at the flare ship, hitting its barrel of flares and causing an explosion that destroyed aircraft and crew.

We spent the rest of the night trying to pull out troops from the north side and waiting until dawn for another frontal assault. The assault met with no resistance because there was no one there except our dead and wounded. My mission for the day was to extract the body bags. No one felt like eating turkey that Thanksgiving Day.

One lesson learned from the Vietnam War that was corrected in later wars –**"It is better to expend bombs that men."**

It was never easy looking at dead soldiers. You impulsively wondered about them and their families. I remember one lad who was on top of an armored vehicle when it ran over a mine. Not a scratch on him--but he was lifeless--a good-looking boy with a wedding ring. I could feel for his young wife.

THE RESCUE MISSION DENIED

On another mission for Colonel Chicken Shit, we were close to an area where a Mohawk aircraft went down just across the river in Cambodia. I asked Chicken Shit if I could drop him off at a firebase so that I could go back and assist with the rescue. He told me, "No." I kept flying in the direction of the crash site and called my operations center for permission to assist with the rescue. The colonel had already called them on his radio in the rear, so they said that they were aware of the situation and could not give me permission to cross the river. I was in sight of the downed aircraft when I observed a jeep with soldiers that I assumed were Cambodians driving toward the aircraft with its crew alongside. I still think I could have made it there in time if I could have put balls-to-the- wall when I first received the call. I hope they made it out safely.

FLYING CIRCLES

Command and Control missions consisted mostly of flying circles in the sky over some kind of combat ground-action. Sometimes it was interesting to listen to the play-by-play assault, but mostly it was boring. We had front row seats to watch air strikes and artillery barrages trying to burn Charlie out of his hiding place, usually a trench line that zigzagged all over. After about six flights of jets dropping napalm, we could make out a trench line. But Charlie always had an escape route if things got too hot. If we ever need to dig another Panama Canal, I suggest we hire some Vietnamese; they are the best damn diggers that I have ever witnessed!

Sometimes, it was obvious that there was nothing developing on the ground but Colonel Chicken Shit still wanted us to remain on station flying in circles anyway. I would reach up and pop my fuel circuit breaker, causing my the low-fuel warning light to blink and my fuel gage would indicate only 200 pounds of fuel (a full tank is 1700 pounds). I would point to the warning light and tell the colonel that we had to head back for more fuel. I didn't abuse this practice but I did use it when it was necessary or someone had to use the latrine.

MEDEVAC AND MY CRASH LANDING

Wear and tear was the other enemy: aircraft fatigue and dust in our air intake, coupled with high heat and high-air density, made a weak ship even weaker. There were days when you could not take off from a three-foot hover and still carry a full crew. After every other landing, the crew chief would have to climb up to the intake air filters and empty the sand out of them.

Aircraft fatigue was partly responsible for the crash landing I had trying to do a medevac into a B-52 bomb crater in the jungle with 90-foot trees. When I received the emergency call, I asked Colonel Chicken Shit if I could let him off at the firebase below because I needed to lighten the aircraft for a medevac. He refused and told me that once I landed, he would stay with the troops until I could return. I didn't have time to debate, so I attempted to come in over the trees and descend into the crater at one side where the blast from the bomb had blown away the surrounding trees.

A soldier on the ground was trying to guide me down to a clear area when he lost all visibility due to the dust and debris as I descended to about 10 feet off the ground. From there on, I was on my own. Unfortunately, my rear skid landed on a 4-foot stump and as I tried to regain to a level hover, my power just bled off. All I could do was ride it out as I lost torque and spun in the direction of the poor troops resting on the other side of the crater. Ka-bam! I landed with my rotor blades hitting some trees close enough to the troops to get an M-16 rifle barrel stuck into the tail boom. Apparently the owner left it behind as he jumped away from the impending crash. I was just glad I didn't end up in the crater that was about 30 feet in diameter and deep as hell.

Colonel Chicken Shit had the first LOH (Cayuse helicopter) that arrived fly him out; and soon after, another one came in and took out the wounded soldier. My crew and I walked out of the Iron Triangle with the platoon. As I walked out, I saw my helicopter being carried back to base camp hanging from under a Chinook (C-47 tandem rotor helicopter) with the rifle still hanging from the tail boom. Ironically, the next day they presented me with a safety certificate for having flown 1,000 hours incident free, not counting bullet holes. It looks as if I made it just under the wire!

LAST WEEKS WITH COLONEL CHICKEN SHIT

The last few weeks of flying Colonel Chicken Shit were winding down, and I was glad to see the end in sight. A few more small events reconfirmed my opinion of him. One early morning we flew a few clicks to the edge of the Hobo Woods where a firebase had just been hit before dawn. I landed outside the perimeter near a forward outpost where there were several VC bodies lying around. A young soldier, still filled with adrenaline from the earlier events, approached us--excited to tell how his buddy and he had held the position. The colonel--looking angrily at the excited soldier--just said, "Go put your blouse on!" I could feel the disappointment of this young brave man who had expected some form of deserved praise.

On the way back to Dau Tieng, I straightened the colonel's curly hair when I flew over the Hobo Woods at about 600 feet and looked down to see a B-52 strike directly below me. We realized we were in-between the ground and a bomb-bay door. Boy was that a close view! Luckily we just had shock waves from the impact of the big bomb.

Normally, on the emergency band there was always an announcement two minutes prior to the bombing; our timing was such that we had missed the announcement.

One night I was awakened to go fly some barbed wire and radar parts out to a firebase just down river. Just before liftoff I was asked to wait for Colonel Chicken Shit. He finally arrived and we flew our mission. I delivered the barbed wire and, having no further instructions, we flew back to base. I wondered why he came along for the ride.

My curiosity was answered a few days later when the sergeant major asked me if I would write the colonel up for a citation before he left country. In amazement I asked, "For what?" He cited the flight the previous night out to the firebase to deliver emergency supplies. I said, "No way in hell!" I always wondered if the sergeant major had to write it.

NOTE

When I returned to the states as an instructor, I received a call from Colonel Chicken Shit informing me that he was attending a VIP short version of flight training at Fort Wolters, Texas. I wondered if he ever figured out my fuel circuit-breaker trick!

CHAPTER 5

BURNOUT AND BAD NEWS

After Colonel Chicken Shit left, I felt relieved but I also had burnout from this mission. The new colonel seemed very military and friendly but I did not want to be disappointed as I had been before, witnessing poor tactile decisions made on the battlefield. Somehow I felt a part of the process.

After just a few days of flying for the new colonel, my attitude may have caught up with my flying. I dropped the new colonel off on the side of the road that wound through the Michelin Rubber Plantation so that he could view some weapons found stashed among the trees. The dusty road made a right turn at the corner where the stash was found. It would make a good place to ambush a convoy. Just before the road turned, it had been cleared of rubber trees on both sides of the roadway for about 40 feet; then after the turn, there was a canopy of trees over the roadway like a tunnel.

I had to go back to Dau Tieng to refuel and did not want to take off heading downwind along the dusty, cleared road. I elected to go through the tunnel of trees that was bigger than any airport hangar. I slowly followed the arch of trees as it wound its way straight to Dau Tieng. It was beautiful, and toward the end of the tunnel I saw a large opening in the canopy and flew through it. When we popped out of the trees, we were looking at Dau Tieng base camp at the bottom of the hill. We refueled and headed back for the colonel.

The crew talked all the way back about taking the colonel through the tunnel. Again, I really did not want to take off in the other direction because the ground was baked by the sun and a lot dustier; so when the colonel hopped on board, we proceeded to fly through the tunnel. Only now I was a little more confident about the journey and its outcome. As

I increased my airspeed, the colonel started tapping me on the shoulder, wondering if we were going too fast. It was about that time I pulled my cyclic (controls attitude) back and popped out of the trees through the opening in the top of the canopy.

When we landed, I noticed some determination in the colonel's step as he headed for the command bunker. Yes, he called my flight operations and requested another pilot. The funny thing was that he requested my copilot who had been encouraging me to go even faster. But things work out for the best: I was ready for other missions. Once you were in-country over six months, you were considered a "short timer" and had a tendency to be a little cocky. I enjoyed every mission after that until I left on the big bird home

BAD NEWS

One morning I was told to report to Flight Operations, and I was informed that my old roommate at Fort Rucker, Alabama was killed the previous night while flying lead gunship on a combat assault into an area near the Iron Triangle. Apparently it was a night assault where the flight was dropping off Republic of Vietnam Armed Forces (RVNAF) troops. Pete attempted to make one final attack in front of the flight and collided with the lead aircraft that was going in without navigation lights. I had just seen Pete about two weeks before in Saigon when I landed at Red Carpet Pad. He had had his arm in a cast and jokingly mentioned something about falling down drunk; he expected to get back to flying soon.

I still think about old Pete from time to time but especially around my wedding anniversary reminiscing about how Pete introduced me to my wife. He never talked about his parents but I got the impression that there was not a strong family bond. He came home with me on a weekend pass to enjoy some of my mom's Cajun cooking. He was quick to comment to the other pilots about what great food and family I had. I miss him.

During my tour in Nam I don't remember seeing any soldiers laugh and they barely smiled. If you did see someone smiling, it was usually the new guys who still had a real dumb smile on their face, which could change to fear in an instant. New guys were also sweating a lot. Those who were in-country (Vietnam) for a while became acclimated to the heat; they also had blank expressions on their slightly yellow faces. The malaria pills left a definite yellow stain on our skin. Everyone looked jaundiced. The only other people with wet blouses were generals and officers who spent most of their tour in air-conditioned quarters.

In war, silent thoughts about who will live and who will die are not discussed among soldiers, but each of us, at some moment in time, have looked at a fellow soldier's face and wondered if he would be there tomorrow. You quickly blow it off, as a chill goes down your spine, hoping that the feeling was just another stupid thought. You sometimes wonder if you are too compassionate or too cold about such silent thoughts. Right! Real men don't care. The hell they don't!

CHAPTER 6

MY BUDDY, FRED

I didn't always fly C&C missions. When my aircraft was down for maintenance, I flew back to Cu Chi and performed other missions. I actually had three hooches: one in Tay Ninh, one in Dau Tieng, and my main base hooch in Cu Chi. Back in Louisiana we always named our fishing/hunting camps, so I named my hooch Cu Chi Hoochi. My friend, Lieutenant Fred Dickens, named his hooch "The Holiday Inn" and the Holiday Inn Corporation sent him one of their signs to put on top of his hooch.

Fred putting up his sign

Fred was my platoon leader but he flew as my copilot for a while when he first came in-country. I am not sure if he was good luck or bad luck because it seemed that whenever we flew together, it was always an adventure. For example, when we were flying a "flare mission" one dark night near Tay Ninh, we had a new door gunner. His job was to take the three-foot long flare canister out of the flare bucket that was attached to the side of the cargo compartment and set the altitude at which it should ignite. It was extremely important to hold on to the two-foot lanyard before throwing the canister over the side. The canister would release a parachute at the prescribed attitude and then the flare would ignite. The flare would burn brightly as it floated down over the area to be illuminated.

Normally, the door gunner would stick the pointed end of a screwdriver through the ring at the end of the lanyard to prevent injuring his finger. However that procedure required gripping the shaft of the screwdriver on both sides of the ring to keep the ring from sliding off the screwdriver. The new guy forgot to do that and the ring slipped off the screwdriver prematurely.

The canister fell out of the cargo compartment and the lanyard lodged itself onto the base of the gun mounting. Unfortunately, the flare ignited. The light was so blinding that I had to shield my eyes, looking only at my instruments as if I were flying IFR (instruments flying required). I managed to keep us straight and level while Ferguson, my crew chief climbed out onto the skids and managed to dislodge the lanyard from the gun mount. We did not realize until after we landed that the flare had burned a one-foot hole below the engine compartment, about one foot above the fuel compartment. My crew chief saved our lives! Of all the close calls I had in Nam, this one was scary. Helicopters burn fast; the side of the ship was still smoking when we landed. I began to wonder about just how many lives this cat (me) had.

HIGH-OVERHEAD APPROACH

I took pride in training my copilots. As far as I know, they all made it home. I hope I can assume some credit for training them well.

Fred was jokingly retelling the story about one night we were on a counter-mortar mission when I let him make a high-overhead approach to a pad just outside the fire support base perimeter. He said that he was performing the approach perfectly until the last 10 feet when, all of a sudden, the ground moisture, combined with dust, fogged up his windows and he said he thought he would die. And then he said (in Fred's special way), "Like the hand of God, all of a sudden, the collective magically started to rise and we landed safely on the pad." I have never been called a god before; Fred was good at dramatics.

COOL HAND LUKE

Fred Dickens was also somewhat of an instigator. I'm not a heavy drinker; but being reared in New Orleans, I started drinking beer and wine moderately with my first taste of crawfish. One night in Nam, Fred and I went to the outdoor theater to see "Cool Hand Luke." As always, there were some idiots who set off a tear gas grenade. We always carried an orange with us when we went to the theater and spread the juice on our face. It helped prevent the tear gas from burning our skin and even our eyes to some extent.

Coming back from the movie, we stopped at the officers' club for a beer. Fred, thinking about the scene from the movie where Luke ate all the eggs, decided to challenge one of his friends to a bet that I could drink a six-pack of beer in 20 seconds. (Fred had seen me swallow a can of beer in three seconds at the Holiday Inn the week before; Fred was easy to impress.)

The other lieutenant took on the bet for twenty bucks. Before I could protest, they went to get six beers. The club only had keg-beer that night, so the idiots contrived that the jerky-can on the bar was approximately the same volume as six beers. They filled the jerky-can to the brim and handed it to me. I commenced swallowing the whole can of beer and just as the final second ticked off, the young lieutenant standing in front of me started trying to out-scream Fred. He claimed that it took me twenty-one seconds to drink the beer. The residual salt in the jerky-can began to foam inside my stomach and the next moment found the contents of my stomach on the poor lieutenant. In frustration, all he could say was, "Damn! I lost twenty bucks and was thrown-up on in the same night!" Luckily, the beer did not stay in me. I strongly recommend against anyone ever doing that. My dad would have viewed it as a dumb thing to do.

COUNTER-MORTAR MISSION

We only had flown 220 hours in nine months of flight school, but we flew almost that amount monthly in Nam. I flew over 460 night-hours where each night-hour represented pure action. The most common night mission was counter-mortar. The purpose of the mission was supposed to be looking for enemy mortar sites by seeing the flash they made as they were launched, or better yet, the rocket launches which looked like roman candles but sounded like low-flying jets. There were always mortars being launched at us at night to psych us out; but the mission was mostly flying emergency re-supply and medevac for everybody after normal business hours.

Fred Dickens invited me to fly with him on his counter-mortar mission as his copilot one night. It was one of those exciting evenings where Firebase Diamond was under attack. It had all the elements I mentioned before--anti-aircraft fire, etc. We were requested to land at the firebase to drop off some ammo. Making a wide circle, low-level over an area that we presumed to be friendly territory, we approached in pitch-of-night blackness at what we thought was the firebase. On final approach we flared the aircraft (slowed down our airspeed by raising the nose of the aircraft and pushing down on the collective to maintain a low altitude). About that time, the troops turned on at least six strobe lights that looked exactly like rifle muzzle flashes. Oops! Is that enemy fire?

Fred started to pull power to do a go-around and I was pushing down on the collective because I felt that it was too late, that we were committed. But, just in case, I unlashed my gun holster and confirmed that my .45-caliber was available if needed. We landed just outside the perimeter next to an APC--so close that the tank's antenna was less that a foot from my rotor blade. The crew chief jumped off and unloaded the ammunition. We were back in the air before the enemy could lock in on us; however, the firebase called us the minute we were airborne to tell us that we forgot our crew chief. No problem, since we had to go back with some more ammo anyway. We could pick him up on the return trip; he should be safe until we landed again.

We were instructed to go to another firebase to pick up more ammo and return. On the high-overhead approach to the other firebase, just as we flared the aircraft to slow it down, we turned on our landing lights and were surprised to see VC bodies in front of us and in the perimeter wire. I called the unit and told them politely that when they came under an attack, it would have been nice to let us know. (They almost gave us a heart attack!) We loaded up and went back to pick up our crew chief and drop off some more goodies.

FRED'S HONEYMOON AFTER THE WAR

Fred and I also laugh about the reunion we had after we both got back from Nam. Fred came down to New Orleans on his honeymoon and we went out to eat at the old Tchoupitoulas Plantation Restaurant. Both of us had been away from the real world for quite awhile, and I don't mean just Nam. We were used to the prices at the officers' clubs in which you could get a gourmet dinner for ten bucks per person. We each ordered duck d'orange but the price was not on the menu. We were initially fighting over who was going to pay the bill until it came, and then we really began to laugh: between the two of us, we had only twenty-five cents left for the tip.

CHAPTER 7

MY PURPLE HEART

Courier missions were daytime Nam-UPS (dropping off personnel and supplies). It was a break from the war. Lie back and listen to FM music. The courier mission was a good mission to train a copilot on--allowing him to learn the area and fly. It was a fun mission; if we got lucky, we might even get the opportunity to have a round eye Red Cross lady "Donut Dolly" or a nurse as a passenger. It was just safe, daytime flying up into the clouds and landing or takeoffs from real concrete helipads.

Typically, the first sortie (first leg of flight) was to fly to Saigon to pick up some new guys and introduce them to their new home, Nam. It was a tradition on my ship to detour on the return trip from Saigon and fly over to the Arps (a savanna, marsh) to test fires our weapons. That gave the new guys something to write home about on their first day. It was always interesting to see their reactions, besides scaring the hell out of them, when both of my door gunners would open fire at the gooney birds feeding in the tall marsh grass. After we landed, some of our passengers responded by giving us the thumbs up, some of them came over to give me a high-five, but there were others who would really be ticked off and wave their middle finger. If looks could kill!

Sometimes even routine missions could end up exciting. The day I was wounded was one such day. Usually, the last mission of the day was dropping off hot food canisters to troops in the field; however, on my last sortie I was asked to land at a reconnaissance patrol location to pick up some POWs.

It was near dusk when I arrived in the area but still daylight enough for them to pop smoke for recognition. There were no less than three different locations with smoke rising from the hedgelines. Obviously Charlie was monitoring our frequency, so I asked them to come up a nickel and a dime on their Fox Mike (.15 MHz). They came up to the new frequency and I asked them to pop smoke again. I visually confirmed with them that it was green smoke. I circled to begin my approach; it was already dark as I made my final approach. I turned on my searchlight at about 100 feet and saw American troops crouched behind rice paddy dikes, so I immediately turned the lights off. I landed in the typical rice paddy with hedgelines on all sides.

Once I landed, a soldier jumped on board with his POW whose hands were tied behind his back and a sandbag was over his head. Another POW was coming toward our ship when all hell broke loose! Tracers were coming from the right hedgeline so I pulled pitch (power to get lift) just as an APG round (VC bazooka) came across my bow, glowing like a Roman candle. As I was about 20 feet above the ground several rounds hit my ship.

One armor-piercing round came through the panel behind my copilot, missing his head about three inches, and then entered my helmet on the right side and went out the left side, finally exiting through the upper left door panel. The impact was as if someone hit me with a baseball bat. I was knocked forward and my helmet fell to the floor. For a moment I thought the prisoner had escaped and hit me with a gun butt. I managed to regain my senses enough to pull back on the cyclic (controls attitude) and hop over what I thought, in the dark, was a tree.

Bullet Hole (in) Helmet

I looked over at my copilot who was not on the controls with me; he was too busy looking out the window at all the pretty fireworks. After climbing to a safe altitude, I fumbled to find my helmet on the floor.

And finally, I could talk on the intercom and request my copilot take the controls. I reported back to the guys on the ground and advised them to hold the other prisoner until daylight. It was then I felt some fluid running down my face and realized that I was injured. Apparently the shattered glass from my visor pitted my face and the bullet slightly grazed the side of my head.

I debated with my crew if it were serious enough to make a stop at the medevac pad. They talked me into going to the hospital where the medics cleaned me up and applied a big band-aid. When my crew chief brought in my helmet with the bullet holes on both sides, the doctor at once realized what a close call I had had. The doctors pushed a straight wire through the holes in my helmet. The bullet's trajectory should have gone through my temples but the impact of the bullet moved my helmet forward enough so that it only grazed my skull. One of the doctors was documenting all the close calls he had witnessed in the MASH unit and asked if I would come back the next day so he could take photos

The full impact of what had taken place did not really hit me until 20 years later, when I happened to look at my award of the Purple Heart and realized that the date was the same as my son's birth date--but three years after I was wounded, August 14, 1968. If I had had a little more airspeed or if I had crouched forward a little more, perhaps my son Clint would not exist. Scratch another cat-life!

Bullet Hole (out) of Helmet

CHAPTER 8

MY BEST DAY IN NAM

My best day in Nam was when I was flying in support of a fire support base near the Cambodian border. It was one of those mornings with low ceiling (cloud cover) of 600 feet but reports of blue sky above 1,000 feet. No big deal: I was never grounded due to weather in Nam! I had the same copilot that I had when I was wounded a week before; we took off ascending into the clouds and climbed out on top of the clouds at 900 feet. Looking ahead at the blanket of clouds we flew southwest above the clouds

Flying toward the general location of the ground unit, I called them on the Fox Mike and, using my directional finder, homed in on their location. I asked how high the cloud cover was and they said about 200 feet. As long as it was above the height of the trees I could make it into their location. Turning with the needle on the direction-finder and descending, we broke out of the clouds at 200 feet, looking straight ahead at a normal- approach landing on the roadway just outside their barbed wire. A sergeant came out to meet us and invited us in for coffee. He said that his lieutenant and he would fly with us to observe the troops sweeping the area toward a small village down the road.

As soon as the clouds lifted I pulled pitch and flew over the road, catching up with the platoon as they approached the village. The road intersected another road at the foot of the village. As we crossed over the huts that were lined up single file along the intersection, I noticed some men in black pajamas with weapons crouching around one man who was pointing as if he were giving instructions to them.

I alerted the gunner and dove in a steep turn toward the VC, with both door gunners firing ahead of the aircraft at the group of VC. Our troops on the ground dove for cover on both sides of the road. My guests in the cargo compartment were startled by the sudden commotion since they were not connected to our intercom; however, the sergeant caught on quickly and also started firing at the enemy. Each time I made a radical maneuver, the sergeant in the cargo compartment would strafe my rotor blades as he continued firing his M-16 while falling backwards. I was just relieved that he put away his M-79 grenade launcher and was only firing his M-16. My copilot also shot a hole in my skid with his .45-calilber. I'm not sure how many holes in my aircraft were from the enemy and how many were from friendly fire.

The enemy scattered; most of them were heading west toward the river. We were now flying low-level, less than a hundred feet, looking over the bamboo hedge line that outlined each rice field, looking for VC. I spotted one lying in the prone position (face down/on his belly). I made a wide turn and came back around, giving instructions to my gunner to point his .60-cal straight down and to fire on my command as we flew over the VC at 10 feet above the ground. Unbelievably, we missed him and when we came back around, he was gone.

We continued to search up and down hedgerows until I spotted three more VC in the prone position, hiding behind a bamboo hedge line overlooking a small rice field in which a patrol of eight soldiers were heading toward them. I did not have much time and I wanted to get it right this time. I turned around, leveling off at 20 feet off the deck, and almost flew into a tree because my head was turned trying to keep my eye on the VC behind us. This time I prepared my gunner to lean out of the aircraft and start firing ahead of the aircraft to give him more time on the target. It worked perfectly; we got all three VC before they could ambush our soldiers.

I flew back to the area where we lost that first VC, but the troops searching the area could not find him. I came around again and dropped smoke in the area we saw him last. In a closer search, the troops found him huddled under some bushes; he was shaking like a leaf and his weapon was jammed. The soldiers later gave me the captured VC's AK-47, with a folding stock, in appreciation for saving their butts. A good day is always one where you saved GIs' lives.

We took the POW aboard and flew him back to our base camp where we went to get fuel. On the way back to the area, the road had VC flags hanging on bamboo every mile. I went low-level and had my door gunner stick out his .60-cal to catch one of the flags on the barrel as a souvenir. After searching the area completely, we flew back to the unit's base camp where I dropped off the sergeant and lieutenant

Prisoners of War

I went to the mess tent for some java; while I was gone someone came up to my crew and asked for everyone's name: A month later while standing in formation, I was amused to see them present my copilot (the 2nd lieutenant) a silver star for our part in that day's events. I realized that someone misunderstood that he might have been the highest-ranking pilot but he was not the aircraft commander. I figured, what the hell!--I was not in the service as a career. The fact is that every crewmember was a part of our success and everyone should have received a commendation medal. There would always be times when you would get a medal for doing a normal mission, and there were times when you wouldn't receive one for a mission on which you really deserved one. It's a fact, Jack, live with it!

MY DFC

I was surprised to receive the Distinguished Flying Cross for a mission I thought was just another typical emergency re-supply night mission. The landing zone was a bit tight but my aircraft did not receive any hits from enemy fire. A patrol was ambushed just before dark and was surrounded in a hamlet west of Cu Chi. They were defending themselves inside a rice farmer's hut within a small perimeter of bamboo and dikes.

I made three landings that night, dropping off ammo and evacuating some wounded into an area so tight that my rotor blades were clipping off the tops of bamboo and palm leaves. On each approach to the LZ, I went in from a different direction because Charlie always tried to cover the previous approach. Luckily, I had just enough moonlight so that I did not have to turn on my searchlights to land. It must have been a tight maneuver since the cheeks of my ass were sore for three days due to the pucker factor.

On one of my flights back to base camp that same night to drop off a wounded soldier, another aircraft beat me to the traffic pattern so I had to follow him on to final approach to the med pad. However, someone had hung new communication wire across the approach end to the medevac pad, causing the helicopter in front of me to trip on the wire and crash in flames on the landing pad. I had to make a go-around; and sadly as I flew over the crash site, I saw one of the crew crawled out of the burning aircraft onto the pad with his clothes on fire, crawling as far as he could away from the burning chopper. What would have happened if I had been first in the traffic pattern? Would I have seen the wire?

Children of Nam

My Mamasan

The Company Area

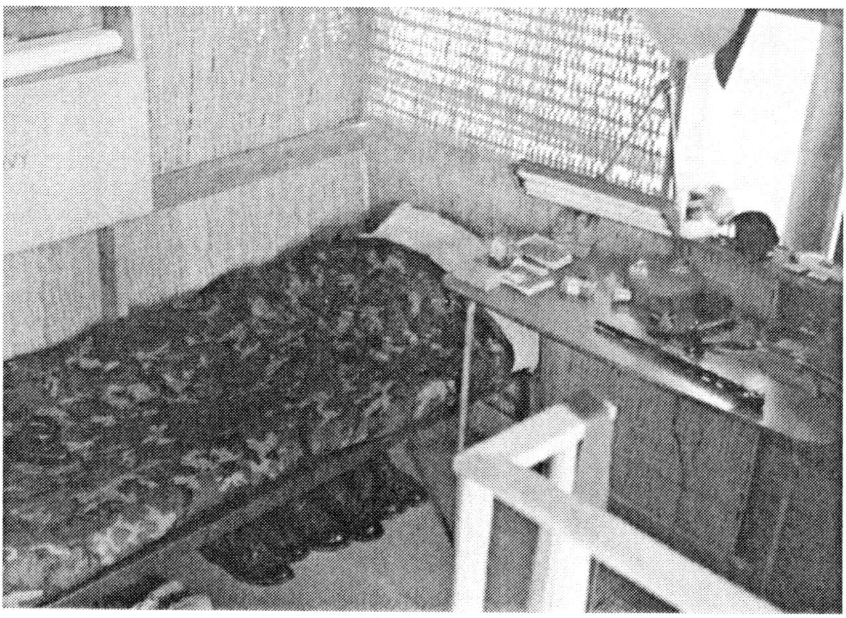

My Quarters

Mister Juge, CW2 and his Aircraft

Village on Hwy. One

CHAPTER 9

MAGNET-ASS

Little Bear aircraft were shot up so much that they looked like hobos with patches, forward and aft. If you received too many hits, you gained a reputation as magnet-ass. It still amazes me how many rounds the Hueys could take and still stay flying. Unless your aircraft was hit in a vital area (like the pilot or flight controls), it kept chugging along. I had .50-cal chew up my main rotor and, although it was a bumpy flight home, it still flew. Even with the tail rotor or hydraulics shot up, could still fly the old Huey. It is the landing that could get tricky.

Bullet Hole in tail rotor drive

One day I received some hits to my tail boom and, after landing, I opened the cowling (a metal cover) for the tail-rotor-drive shaft to see how bad it was. The tail-rotor shaft (which looks like a PVC pipe) was still turning and it appeared not to be in one piece. When the drive shaft finally stopped, I saw that it had a hole the size of my fist, with only a sliver of metal on the top and bottom holding it together. If it had broken apart, the centrifugal force would have caused it to swing wildly and virtually knock off the tail boom. Of course, having no capability of anti-torque control, the aircraft would have spun itself into the ground.

The most important component of the helicopter is its rotor and rotor blades. There is a nut that holds everything together on the top of the rotor called the Jesus nut; if that nut falls off--you get to see Jesus. I realized how vulnerable the helicopter rotors really were when a Mayday came over the emergency band one day. "Mayday! Mayday! This is Greyhound 26. I have just slung a rotor blade (The rotor blade had fallen off.) and I'm going down in grid 12----84." Pause. "Disregard medevac." My copilot and I just turned and looked at each other. Yes, it was for real and yes, he did not need a medevac, he knew he was going to die. Choppers can't fly without its pair of rotors. But it was the bravest thing I had ever heard! Greyhound 26 had remained as calm as if it were a minor annoyance. I believe I would have lost it. I would be cursing army maintenance all the way down.

MIND GAMES

The last time that Fred and I had a chance to fly together was January 25, 1969. He asked if I would fly as his copilot on what was supposed to be a quiet day. We left Cu Chi at daybreak and flew a few routine missions when Flight Operations called and chewed us out for having two aircraft commanders on the same flight. It seemed that we were still in the residual counterattacks from the TET offensive and Charlie was again on the offensive. So we flew back to home base and I jumped into another aircraft to take a different mission. Less than one hour later, I got the word that the other pilot who had taken my position as copilot was wounded but the aircraft was flyable and Fred was able to return to base safely.

I cannot remember all that we did that day except we never shut down even to refuel and I ended up flying the longest day that I had ever flown in Nam. We logged a total of twenty-two hours of flight time from seven A.M. on January the 25th to five A.M. the next day. At midnight I would celebrate my twenty-fifth birthday. The day seemed even longer since I had a deep-rooted feeling before I left for Nam that perhaps I would not see my twenty-fifth birthday.

We ate C-rations and relieved ourselves when we stopped to refuel. This was SOP (standard operating procedure) for pilots in Nam. As the mission extended past dark, the sleep factor always began to wear at my consciousness. Flying circles over fire-support Base Diamond with a sky full of bullets, aircraft, and smoke, waiting to be called to make a delivery, made a boring night. We were not at immediate risk from the enemy as much as we were from ourselves. Even taking turns at the stick and trying to close your eyes for a few minutes, you could never really go to sleep for fear that your copilot might fall asleep while flying. All I could do was rest my eyes--not my mind.

It was a scary feeling, when my eyelids got heavy and my head would periodically jerk up as I strained to maintain consciousness. I was constantly trying to convince my subconscious not to submit to thoughts about closing my eyelids, for just a few seconds. I had to constantly shake my head and change positions in the seat to stimulate my consciousness. At one point, I looked up and thought I saw the outline of a Cobra helicopter just in front of us and I made a radical turn to avoid contact. I don't know if it was really there, but I did succeed in waking everyone for the rest of the night.

As it approached midnight, I began to think about my fear of an early death and I really wanted to call it a night. But there was no relief: an hour before midnight I was called to go to a village north of Cu Chi and land on a muddy road inside the village. This was the kind of landing I would be leery about doing in broad daylight--but I was nervous as hell about landing there at night because the village was normally infiltrated with VC. I called the ground troops who were in the village and they guided me down to the road. There were some phone lines hanging across the road that no one had mentioned but we managed to avoid them. I picked up one wounded and one KIA and flew back to my main base camp, dropping them both off at the medevac pad.

Returning to my assigned circle in the sky over Firebase Diamond, I felt relieved that it was now my birthday and I could relax. However, a sleepy mind is one full of mischief and I started asking myself if my thoughts of dying were misinterpreted. Perhaps my premonition applied to the day of my twenty-fifth birthday. I resolved to try to stay alive for at least another twenty-four hours and get this monkey off my psychological back.

The last five hours were active as we watched Quad-50's (anti-aircraft gun emplacements) trying to pick off the aircraft flying above them. The jets (nicknamed "Stovepipes" by helicopter pilots, since all that was visible at night was a flame coming out of a flying tube) gave a great show as they dove at the enemy positions, dropping napalm, lighting up the area like a ball from hell as the jelly-fuel ignited. As the jets pulled up, all that was visible were the afterburners glowing red as a long flame followed after them, straight up.

We flew in and out of the firebase without receiving any hits and I must have passed the sleep barrier because I was a lot more alert the rest of the night. As dawn came, the battle was over and we headed home. I don't think anyone in Flight Operations realized how many hours we had flown since Flight Operations had changed shifts three times since I saw them last. But I did spend the rest of my birthday sleeping. Once I awoke, I never again thought about dying: the monkey was off my back and I could get on with my missions.

WHY WORRY!

We had a saying in the Army if we were concerned about screwing up: "What's the worst that can happen? They might send you back to Nam?" After Nam, every problem seems trivial. My approach to life since Nam has been, that there are some things you can do something about and other things you have no control over; so why worry. I carry jokes in one pocket and a sense of humor in the other, along with proverbs and wise sayings. I believe that Anonymous is the wisest person on earth and that we should seek his advice. I enjoy pondering the truisms from sayings of unknown authors who seem to have more insight to life than most.

If I have a debt or deadline to meet, I am reminded of the story Anonymous told about the king who called in his magician and told him of his deep love for his horse. He wanted to be able to talk to his horse and have his horse reply. He further demanded that if he could not magically help his horse talk, he would immediately cut off the magician's head. The magician naturally said that it could be done but something of this nature would take some time. The king said he would give him two months to accomplish the deed or suffer the consequences. As the magician was walking out, his aide asked how he could be smiling, knowing that in two months he would die? The magician replied that he was alive today and that in two months the king could be dead, he could be dead, or the horse could be dead--or the horse might start talking. Why worry?

CHAPTER 10

EXTRA DUTIES

Sometimes when I flew too many hours, I would be grounded for a few days and would have to return to the company area. My XO and I did not get along well; he had a nitpicking personality. He would get onto me for not wearing the official company baseball cap; I liked wearing my jungle hat with one side up. It seemed that he would go out of his way to assign me some crappy duties around the company area in my free time. I blame Colonel Chicken Shit and him for my bad attitude toward authority figures. But one time he screwed up and gave me a job I actually enjoyed--building a better cage for our mascot, Spooky (a Japanese sun bear), that had been confined to a small 6 x 12 foot cage.

I was provided four hooch maids (mamasans) to dig a chain wall around the 20 x 20 perimeter to prevent the bear from digging his way out. I also had a large hole dug as a small pond for the bear to cool off in. I had an old tree trunk flown in by chopper and planted it in the ground for the bear to climb. I tied an old tire on a rope and hung it from the tree so Spooky could bop it around and play. A large metal culvert, cut in half, acted as a bunker for the bear. The bunker roof and insides of the water pond were cemented. The hurricane fence installed around the perimeter and roof prevented the bear from climbing out. The bear was introduced to his new home in the center of the company square. He seemed to like it and it prevented him from escaping to ransack the company area.

About every sixty days I had to pull bunker-line duty-officer. Our unit was responsible for defending the southeast corner of the base camp that protected two vital areas--the POL (aviation fuel depot) and the revetment area (parking area) of the big CH-47 Chinook tandem-rotor helicopters. Our area of responsibility was at least 2500 feet of the perimeter. We had two attempts of enemy penetration through our defenses while I was in Nam.

My job was to periodically walk the line of bunkers to check on the men in to see if they were awake and if they had seen any movement. The bunkers were just outside a mud revetment (we call them levees back in Louisiana), surrounding the fuel dump and aircraft to prevent personnel in that area from receiving enemy fire. Some of the men on bunker-line duty were our crew chiefs and door gunners; I had a lot of faith in them because of their past performance.

Unfortunately, some of the soldiers assigned to that duty were awaiting orders for disciplinary action. Naturally, I kept a closer eye on their bunkers. I had to constantly remind them not to smoke their cigarettes in the open since Charlie could see that glow for quite a distance. You would think that self-preservation would be incentive enough for them to cover the glow by cupping their cigarettes in the palm of their hand!

To get from one bunker to the next I had to walk on top of the levee. Back and forth, back and forth, I felt like a duck in a shooting gallery. We had the "Starlight scope" which gave you just enough night vision for your imagination to play hell with your mind. There were always some animals (huge rats, and dogs) in the barbed wire rattling the cans hanging on the wire, just enough to keep you on your toes all night.

I amused myself making pinch pottery from the muddy clay at my feet while awaiting first light. I made a mental commitment to take up pottery-making as a hobby when I returned home, which I did thirty years later. I wanted to stay reminded of these times and keep humble--knowing that we shall all return to the earth and mix with the mud someday.

The poor troops in the field would also have to take turns pulling bunker-line duty every night and still have to walk into the jungle every morning on patrols looking for the enemy or enemy ammo stashes. Naturally, the troops in the field would eventually relax their guard after many nights of no action, and that was when Charlie would attack. We were primarily fighting North Vietnamese soldiers by 1968 since, by attrition, we had virtually annihilated the original South Vietnamese resistance.

The North Viet Cong would normally concentrate their efforts around Tet (Vietnamese New Year) and employ smaller forces during the rest of the year, taking turns attacking one firebase at a time. Our search-and-destroy missions were designed primarily to detect such movements and the build-up of enemy troops and supplies. Our forces were somewhat restricted during the wet season, preventing us from using our tanks, or even the armored personnel carriers, off the main roads. So it was not the kind of war where our soldiers had contact with Charlie every day. You never knew when or where the next attack would come, and it played on one's nerves.

BAD DAYS

I have had a few bad days where I wondered if I could have done more. I remember being called up to do a medevac a few clicks (kilometers) from my position. We landed on a dirt road along the Song Saigon River near Dao Tieng to evacuate some troops who had hit a mine with their armored personnel carrier. A couple of them were obviously in bad shape and were loaded aboard, but one GI was walking around holding his ears and refused to get on our aircraft. I could not wait any longer so I pulled pitch and flew low-level up the road under the canopy of trees, straight to Dao Tieng. After dropping off the wounded, I flew back to find that the young soldier who had refused to board. I learned, sadly, that he had collapsed and died. He apparently had some internal bleeding which no one detected.

SOMETHING TO FEEL GOOD ABOUT

Sometimes little things can make your day! One night I flew back to Dau Tieng just as the heavy fog rolled into the valley. After refueling, I hovered back to my helipad and heard a Bird Dog pilot (fixed wing aircraft) talking to the ground flight controller about his dilemma. Circling above the unlit field, he did not see the airstrip and was running low on fuel. I assisted him by hovering at the end of the airstrip with my landing light pointed down the runway. He flew just over my rotor head as he ran out of fuel but was able to glide to a safe landing. He bought the beer that night!

TRAINING PILOTS

I was always training pilots. It was a secondary but very important duty of aircraft commanders. Anyone who has flown in combat knows it's always hard to relinquish the controls to another pilot, especially a new one. The first few that I trained were the lucky ones--before my patience ran out. I soon realized that a new pilot could get you killed! Some of them commented to me that I was a bit of a hard ass, but at least they were alive to tell me.

There was one incident when I grounded a pilot, and now I feel guilty about that in retrospect. We were doing a fast, high overhead approach to a firebase when my copilot suddenly grabbed his head. For a moment I thought he took a round, but it turned out to be a sinus headache. I shook my head, thinking that I could not live with this situation in a combat zone where rapid altitude changes are standard procedures. I had him grounded and they made him maintenance officer.

I should have been more sympathetic. A few years later I suffered a similar experience while flying for the Louisiana National Guard on a trip back from San Antonio, Texas. Descending from 4,000 feet to the New Orleans Lake Front Airport, I thought my eyes would pop out of my head and my sinus cavities would implode. I still suffer today when flying on commercial airlines as they descend to land.

THE EMERGENCY FREQUENCY

The emergency frequency was used primarily to announce to the world a major emergency in the air so that other aircraft in the area could respond to the situation. However, every once in a while you hear something funny. One such time was when an unknown aircraft flew over the south end of the runway at Cu Chi. The Airfield tower requested over the emergency band, "Aircraft south of Cu Chi, What are your intentions?" The reply came from the unidentified aircraft, "Honorable!" The perfect answer! I wish I thought of it myself.

CHAPTER 11

CREW CHIEF AND DOOR GUNNER

The crew chief and door gunner were key members of my crew. I was fortunate to have good ones most of the time. I am ashamed that I cannot remember all their names. The military made us lazy when it came to remembering names because we all wore name-tags. You became accustomed to just looking at their pocket for their name. First names were seldom used due to military protocol. (To this day I have a hard time remembering names; and in my business of insurance sales, that's a disadvantage.)

CREW CHIEF

Crew chiefs always stayed with their assigned aircraft, but they also acted as our secondary door gunner while in flight. They were responsible for all the aircraft maintenance, including intermediate (every 25 hours) and periodic (every 100 hours) inspections. Considering that there were many times when we flew an average of 12 hours a day, my crew chief was performing intermediate inspections every other day. That meant that after we came in from a day's mission, the crew chief would have to stay with the helicopter and pull the magneto plugs, change the oil, and complete the inspection so that the aircraft would be ready to fly the next day.

I tried to help one of my crew chiefs one time but I stripped a magneto plug, damaging the engine block so that it required a new engine. I was never invited to help again. The crew chiefs even waxed the ship every time we were on the ground waiting in between missions. It was like taking care of their old Chevy Bellaire. You could always assume that if the crew chief flew with you, it was a flyable aircraft. But it was even more comforting to see him treat it like his baby.

My different Crew Chief

DOOR GUNNER

The primary door gunner was a "grunt" (infantry weapons specialist). It was his responsibility to maintain the aircraft's weapons and provide cover-fire in a hot LZ. I had one gunner we called "Miller the Killer" who had 23 confirmed kills, not all from my aircraft. It takes a lot of skill to be able to lead your target from a moving aircraft, even with tracers. The bullet's trajectory was an arc that ran to the rear of the aircraft. Night firings were impressive to see; however, continuous firing caused the .60-cal barrel to glow red. The door gunner always carried a heavy glove that he used to change barrels when the barrel got too hot. Normally, the gunner asked permission to fire but there were many times when it was obvious. Another good book written by a door gunner from our unit, but in 1966, is HIGEST TRADITIONS by Tony Lazzarini. He describes their mission from a different perspective.

A good door gunner did not have a happy trigger-finger. It was important to be able to confirm whether the target was friend or foe. The door gunner's favorite mission was "firefly"--where we flew along the rivers at night with a Zeon light looking for sampans (Vietnamese boats) to shoot. It was always a thrill to see secondary explosions because then we knew that we had prevented a shipment of explosives from being used against us later.

Both door gunner and crew chief were exposed to the elements and enemy fire as they sat perched on the side of the aircraft with only a chicken board (very small bulletproof vest) for them to hide behind. The pilot, at least, had an armored seat that gave him some comfort, knowing that his family jewels were protected. The flight crew had no choice as to which pilot they drew. I admired their willingness to fly with us at the pick-of-the-draw. Personally, I did not feel comfortable flying unless I was at the controls.

I always felt bad about the fact that the aircraft commander and co-pilot sometimes received a medal when the rest of the crew did not. Everyone on board was important to each mission and everyone took the same risks. I always conferred with my crew before taking on a dangerous mission. I never expected them to vote no, but I wanted them to know that they, also, confirmed that it was a crew effort.

THE VIETNAMESE PEOPLE

I have always admired the Vietnamese people. Most were hard working farmers trying to scratch an existence out of a muddy field. They constantly amazed me with their innovative use of any materials available to them. A brass shell from a 105-cannon round would be transformed into a beautiful vase. Watching the care they displayed in simply wrapping an object in newspaper appeared to me as another one of their expressions of art. Stopping at a small village, I observed a mamasan carefully sweeping the dirt floor of her hut with more care than I have ever seen State-side.

The women were small-boned, slender and very graceful--dressed in long black trousers made of silk, with a companion, lightweight tunic. A majority of the women had long black hair and seemed almost childlike, even at an older age. I tried to explain what snow was to my mamasan, (not that I have seen a lot of it myself). I opened the freezer and scooped up some frosted ice and said, “Snow, same same.” She just giggled, covering her mouth with her small hand and said, “Dinky dau!” which loosely meant—“Crazy GI.”

Also, the women were amazed that the American soldier treated them with respect, which was not a common custom among their Vietnamese men. The girls were not thought to be of any significant value; that only the male child was an asset and he would also receive all inheritance. This fact puzzled me since I observed that it was mostly women in the fields planting rice, not men.

It was unlikely that I could correctly guess the age of a Vietnamese woman beyond thirty years old. I have no idea to this day how old my mamasan was. I only know that she was older than me. It may sound insulting but their society did not believe in "Ever So-Soft" products. Hard work and sun take their toll on the women of Vietnam. I never saw a fat Vietnamese; heart disease was not the number-one killer in their country.

One day I gave my mamasan some money and asked her to go out and buy a Vietnamese dress for my wife so I could mail it home. I gave her an approximate height by pointing to my shoulder. I assumed that since Anzia was thin by American standards it would all work out somehow. Mamasan proudly returned with an outfit that she purchased from the market in Saigon. She was proud that she got the opportunity to purchase such a quality item in the open market for all to see. I sent it home and excitedly awaited a joyful response from my wife who, of course, was quite pregnant at that time. Well, she never replied; so I let dead dogs lie until I got home and found out it wasn't even close to her size! We saved it for our daughter to wear some day to the Mardi Gras. It never happened.

Vietnamese kids would always run up to our aircraft when we landed at a village. They all were streetwise, or should I say paddy-wise? It just seemed that they were a lot wiser, not smarter, than kids the same age back home. We always kept extra cans of C-rations on board our ship to hand out but we were careful not to create a mob scene. I was always glad to get candy from home so I could share with the kids.

CHAPTER 12

SPECIAL ASSIGMENTS

One of the most interesting special missions that I had was flying for the Navy Seals. I arrived at a Republic of Vietnam National Armed Forces (RVNAF) outpost near the Mekong River. It was just a typical small compound with bunkers and lots of barbed wire. I landed just outside the wire and walked through an opening in the layered wire, and minefields and entered the main compound. The outer ring of bunkers was for the South Vietnam troops and the inner circle held the Navy Seals. The Seals had claymore mines facing the RVNAF bunkers in case there were enemy saboteurs among the AVNAF troops. There was a large balloon flying over the command bunker, acting as a high antenna for their radios.

A bearded colonel approached me; that was very unusual--even for Nam--but otherwise he appeared very military. The rest of his troops were the most unmilitary personnel I have ever seen. There was a very large guy who weighed about 280 pounds and had a mustache that stuck out like a walrus'. Of course, they all had tattoos and were dressed in black pajamas and had bandoleers across their chests.

After a cup of the worst java I ever had, my crew and I boarded the chopper with the colonel and five of his men. They instructed me to cross the river into Cambodia and pointed out an area where they wanted me to look for an opening in the trees and then land. Two Diamond Head gun ships came on station to provide cover as we made our approach to the opening. As soon as we landed, the Seals jumped out and secured the area. Two of them went in different directions to place dog-balls (sensors that looked like a dog's balls) on tree branches along a trail. When they returned, they stopped just long enough to remove the leaches from their legs before jumping on board. We made a couple more stops and then landed in a rice paddy where they dug a hole to deposit a long tube-like object with a whip antenna. I suppose it was designed to pick up any signals that the dog-balls sent, detecting motion in the area, and then transmit the signals back to the Seals' compound.

The Navy was responsible for patrolling movement along the rivers between Cambodia and Vietnam and they had several gunboat-patrols all the way up to Tay Ninh. It was always tricky to land on the boat's deck; but the rewards were worth it because the Navy was always good about providing us with a free box of steaks.

Another special mission I had was to support the LRPs (long range patrols). I was told to pick up a rope ladder at Tay Ninh and fly to a given quadrant. Once I was on station, I called a frequency and was given further instructions to hover over the top of some trees (where green smoke had been popped) and lower the rope ladder. I hovered for quite awhile before I felt a tug on the right side of the ship. Up came the LRPs, one by one, climbing on board--some of the ugliest, most ragged-looking troops I ever saw. One of them had a necklace of human ears around his neck! I flew them back to base camp where they drank beer and raised hell until they tired of rules and regulations and soon went back to the jungle to do their thing.

Another impressive operation in Nam was the Rome-Plow Mission where the Army decided to remove the jungle instead of constantly bombing it. The Rome-plow was a huge, M5 front-end bulldozer with a metal canopy plus a wire mesh screen surrounding the driver's compartment to protect the driver from exploding mines and falling trees. There was always another soldier with an automatic weapon who rode shotgun next to the driver.

Normally, groups of fifteen to twenty plows would start cutting away at the area to be defoliated--like Hobo Woods. The lead plow would cut only four feet into the jungle. Each consecutive plow behind would cut the next four feet of jungle. Eventually, the line of plows had cut a square out of the jungle and worked its way inward until the square was void of trees. For encampment at night, the Rome-plows would form a circle facing outward, using their metal plow blades as a shield against enemy fire. Of course, in-between the plows were some armor support for returning fire.

At night when I would fly supplies to the camp, I could see the welders with their cutting torches working--sharpening and repairing the plows for the next day's run at the jungle. You can only imagine the size of these huge mahogany trees that the plows were mowing down. Seventy to eighty feet tall--the trees were pushed over by plows twice the size of my helicopter. They made it seem so easy. I don't recall having heard of any VC ever attacking the Rome-plows. I think all the plows would have to do would be crank up the engine and run over the enemy. If I had not been a helicopter pilot, I think I would have enjoyed driving the big cats.

DEFOLIATE WHAT!

When I first arrived in-country, we had to land and takeoff from the roof of a small bunker located on top of Nui Ba Den. Landing challenged the pilot's skills as the helicopter touched down on a perch not much wider than the skids. But it was like riding a zephyr, when the pilot had to literally dive off the mountain to gain airspeed to fly.

Clouds seemed to linger around the top of the mountain as if the pointed boulders on top of the mountain snagged the passing blanket of moisture. They were always a contributing factor when landing or taking off. After the massacre on top of Nui Ba Den, I described in the second chapter, it was realized that an improved landing pad was needed to be able to protect the troops stationed on the mountain. The new replacement platoon on the mountain immediately cleared an area and made a real landing pad that actually allowed transitional lift (a cushion of air between the ground and aircraft) before leaving the mountain. This new landing pad provided quick emergency support to the unit, even in poor weather.

I had the unique mission one time to defoliate Nui Ba Den. Whoever came up with this brainstorm is one person whose ass I would like to kick. Flying slow and low around a mountain made it impossible for the Cobra gunship to provide proper cover for us. I could see openings in the mountain behind boulders; and you would never be able to convince me that Charlie did not at one time or another, have us in his gun sites. I only knew my chicken board was too small to hide behind. The gunship would have been providing fire support only after the fact--the fact that we would be dead! The Cobra pilot would only be seeking revenge in a counter-attack effort.

Why Charlie didn't take advantage of our vulnerability, I will never know. Perhaps he felt sorry for us or he was concerned about revealing his cave entrance. Charlie was, in all probability, on R&R and said, "The hell with it; I'm on vacation!

Anyhow, the Agent Orange we sprayed over the area never even singed the canopy of mountain scrub brush. And I think that napalm just made it grow faster by killing off contenders for nutriments among the rocks. Nui Ba Den was an impressive pile of rocks, and I miss watching the sunsets and sunrises with old Nui in the background.

Top of Nui Ba Den

CHAPTER 13

INCOMING MORTARS

Anywhere in Nam you were subject to being fired upon by enemy mortars. But after you were in-country for a while, it became less frightening to hear the "incoming."

Charlie would pop the rounds into base camps to psychologically harass us in our sleep; incoming during daylight hours was rare. When I first arrived, I (like everyone else) would scramble in my skivvies on my knees out the door of my hooch and run to a bunker. When you entered a bunker, you didn't want to be first because you might walk into a mouthful of cobwebs. Also, there were reports of some bunkers being booby- trapped by the Vietnamese who worked on base during the day. Thirdly, the bunkers were usually wet--especially during the rainy season--and cold as a witch's tit. Normally, the bunker could repel a mortar but probably not a rocket if it were a direct hit.

The last time I ran to the bunker, I accidentally hit my brand-new wristwatch against the door in a rush to get out of my hooch. I had saved for two months to buy that watch which had an altimeter. Actually, it was the last watch I ever owned.

I was so outraged at the loss of the watch that I decided to build my own personal bunker two feet from my cot. In my free time I cut a 3 x 4-foot opening in the plywood floor, formed the opening, and started to dig. I figured if Charlie could dig huge tunnels to house an army, I should be able to dig a deep pit. If I took a direct hit, it was just meant to be. I dug a hole that was six feet deep and then I dug a tunnel to one side.

One day after coming in from a flight, I noticed that my bunker's trap door was open. When I looked down, I saw my mamasan diligently digging in the pit. She exclaimed, "Tunnel number one!" I think she liked the idea that during the day while I was flying, she could use it herself if some rounds came into the base camp.

One night, a runner from Flight Operations came to my doorway and just before he could step closer to awake me, I jumped up and told him to stop--to prevent him from stepping into the open hole. He was grateful that I was a light sleeper. I decided to keep the lid closed after that: I might forget some night while making a trip to the crapper.

I didn't have a personal pit to jump into at Dau Tieng or Tay Ninh. One night some rockets came into Tay Ninh base camp and we all rolled off the cots and headed for the door on our knees. I had a new copilot, Doug, who was also very new to country. He rolled out of his cot and began crawling on the floor headed for the door but ran into the adjacent wall. He fell back and proceeded to do the same thing again and this time hit the wall even harder. Before he could hit his head again, I grabbed him by his belt and pulled him over to the doorway where he, without skipping a beat, continued to scramble to the bunker. He ended up with a nasty knot on his head, but he was lucky that he hadn't given himself a concussion.

CHAPTER 14

GOING HOME

The last month in Nam I kept busy flying: it helped pass the time. I was totally surprised when Fred Dickens ran into my hooch and told me that if I could get to the Red Carpet Pad in the next few hours, I might be able to get an early ride home to the USA. I hated to miss the traditional going-home celebration at the Officers' Club that all short-timers received before they departed. I would miss extending good luck wishes to all my friends that I would be leaving behind.

I also missed the time I would have had to make all the mental adjustments needed before going back home. Changing mental gears from war to home is a challenge for the returning veteran. I had the extra mental load of knowing that I would have to reacquaint myself with a new wife that I had known only twenty-two days before I left for Nam, and now I had an instant family with child. After a year of hanging around the guys, I knew that I was not the perfect domesticated male. The Army did not teach us the proper shutdown procedures for leaving a war. But I looked forward to facing the new challenge.

All of my personal effects were already pre-packed to be shipped so I just had to grab what was left and stuff it in my duffle bag and go. I arrived at the holding company anxious to get my orders to get on the Big Bird. However, I found out why they called it the holding company. The rush and wait philosophy of the Army was alive and well. It was my misfortune to have a whole boatload of Navy seamen arrive at Red Carpet the same day and they had priority over me. I was put on stand-by. I "stood by" for ten days and left Nam the same time I would have if I had not been given the opportunity to be on stand-by. During that frustrating 240 hours of "standing by" I did not have a fresh change of clothes. Even though I showered every night, my TW's (tropical wear, officer brown summer uniform) were starting to stand at attention all by themselves. I spent every day at the airport, so by the time I got to the barracks it was too late to wash them and have them dry enough for me to wear the next day. I was miserable.

The day I departed Vietnam, my body odor was the least of my concerns. I just wanted to get out of Nam. The flight to Nam was a lot shorter than the flight home. Leaving Nam, I had some guilt feelings about leaving a job unfinished: perhaps my flying experience could have saved more lives if I had stayed longer. But the fact remains--anybody can be replaced--as those pilots I left behind proved. Unlike the flight to Nam, on this flight I did not have to look at another soldier and wonder if he would make it—he did. We all did! As the aircraft lifted off the runway there was a sudden roar of applause from the returnees that actually startled me. It was all finally becoming a reality that up to that moment I had only imagined.

We arrived at an Air Force base outside of San Francisco. After waiting in a long line with duffle and flight bag and going through a customs check, I was on my own. I took a taxi to the commercial airport in San Francisco rather than waiting for a military bus.

When I boarded the commercial jet, the pilot was kind enough to give me a seat in first class which was real nice; however, my body odor made me very self-conscious and I spent the duration of the trip squirming in my seat next to a pretty lady; with the air vent on full blast.

I had called home before I flew out of San Francisco so my family could meet me at the airport. For the past ten days, I never knew whether or not they had received the word that my flight would be delayed. When I stepped off the plane, I could see my parents, wife, and baby in front of the line. I didn't know which one to grab first and ended up grabbing them all. It did not really take long for me to get back into the swing of things. Little things like flushing toilets and shaving indoors gave me pleasures that no one in the house could fully realize. I had a tendency to stare at my wife for hours trying to match the still-picture images caught in my mind, now put into motion. I tried to act normal but inside I was laughing as I drove my MGB again. It was like experiencing all these pleasures all over for the first time.

After trying, in two weeks, to visit with everyone I knew in New Orleans, Anzia, baby Allison, and I headed to Alabama to meet all of my wife's family. It would be soon enough that we would report to my next duty station. I was looking forward to setting up house with my new family.

THE LAST LETTER HOME

I have reproduced an unedited form-letter given to me before I left Vietnam that someone in our company created. I thought it might be interesting to view.

ISSUED WITH SOLEMN WARNING

This____Day__________, 19______

TO____

Very soon, ______________________ will once again be in your midst, de-Americanized, demoralized, and dehydrated, but ready once more to take his place as a human being, to engage in life, liberty, and a somewhat delayed pursuit of happiness.

In making your joyous preparations to welcome him back into respectable society, you must make allowances for the crude environment in which he has suffered for the past _____ months. In a word, he may be somewhat Asiaticized, suffering from Viet Cong-itis, or perhaps from too much BA Moui Ba (Booze).

Therefore, show no alarm if he prefers to squat rather than sit on a chair. He may parade around in sandals and a towel, slyly offer to sell cigarettes to the postman, and pick at his food suspiciously as though he thought you were trying to poison him. Don't be surprised if he answers all questions with "I hate this place!" ; "Number one!"; "Number ten!"; or "Sorry bout that." Please be tolerant when he tries to buy everything at half the asking price; accuse the grocer of being a thief; and refuse to enter any establishment that doesn't have steel mesh screens over the doors and windows.

Any of these sights should be avoided since they can produce a state of advance shock: people dancing; children with toy grenades; and round-eyed women. In a relatively short time his profanity will decrease enough to permit him to associate with mixed groups; and soon will be speaking a recognizable form of English. For a while he may complain about sleeping on a spring mattress, and at first may refuse to go to bed without a mosquito net or rifle.

Make no flattering remarks about exotic Southeast Asia, avoid mention of the benefits of overseas duty; the fun sound of monsoon rain on the roof; and above all, ask permission before mentioning food delicacies of the East, such as flied lice (fried rice). The mere reference to any of these subjects may trigger an awesome display of violence.

For the first few months, until he is house-broken, be especially watchful should he be placed in the company of women, particularly one who is young, beautiful, and round-eyed: his first reaction may be to go into a state of catatonic shock. Take advantage of this momentary hesitation and move the young lady out of his reach. Keep in mind that beneath this tanned and rugged exterior there beats a heart of pure gold. Treasure this, for it is about the only thing of value he has left. Treat him with kindness, tolerance, and an occasional fifth of good whisky and you will soon be able to rehabilitate this hollow shell of the man you once knew.

Send no more letters to Vietnam after_______________ for he is leaving the tropics in ___Days and headed for the land of the BIG PX.

HIS FUTURE MAILING ADDRESS WILL BE________________________________.

In witness whereof the party of the first part has duly executed this warning and set his hand here unto.

CHAPTER 15

MY RETURN TO FORT WOLTERS

I was a little disappointed that my next duty station was not Fort Rucker, Alabama since my wife was from Geneva, Alabama and worked at the base as a nurse. Also it would have been nice to continue flying the Huey helicopter or perhaps even to have the opportunity to transition into other aircraft only available at Fort Rucker. However, no such luck: I got stuck with Fort Wolters, Texas!

Anzia and I prepared her trailer so the military could have it moved, and then we packed up my MGB with her and the baby and pointed the car west. After we arrived, I reported to my next assignment as an instructor pilot in, of all things, a TH-55 trainer. Pilots jokingly referred to this plastic helicopter as "Made by Mattel." Big guys like me hate small helicopters.

After a few months my back was acting up so I accepted a ground instructor position. The new position worked out perfectly since my old roommate, Big John, was also assigned to the same department. He had been a medevac pilot in Nam. It was great to see him again and to be able to meet his wife, Dolly. His baby daughter, Susanne, was the same age as my daughter Allison. We spent a lot of weekends together on the nearby lakes camping and sailing.

Returning to Fort Wolters and discovering that my four companions all made it back alive was overwhelming. Although Pat Lawlor was attached to my unit in Nam and we were close friends, but we did not have a lot of time together because we were both flying our asses off as aircraft commanders. The only time we flew together was in a group flight (formation during combat assaults) and then we were in separate helicopters.

John and I took direct commission to first lieutenant when we got back State-side, especially since it did not add to our initial obligation as a pilot. Pat took a direct commission to second lieutenant before he left Vietnam. At the time he accepted, it seemed like a good deal.

On the day after I was promoted from the rank of CW2 to first lieutenant I went to teach my Navigation class to a flight of young second lieutenants. It was raining that morning and I had on my rain coat. As I walked through the group gathered outside the class, one young smart-ass lieutenant called out to me to ask if I was aware that I should always salute a superior officer. I slowly removed my rain coat to display my new silver bar on each shoulder. I didn't have to say a word; the rest of the flight did it for me.

After leaving the service, Pat paid his way to college by flying as a bush pilot in the Yukon, and is now an engineer for Ford Motor Company. John, after trying his hand as an artist, joined the real world to become a contractor in Dallas. Keith Galloway became an educator; he always was the smart, quiet one. Tom Landry--that crazy redheaded woodpecker--no telling what he's doing!

As a ground-school instructor at Fort Wolters, I always began the class by telling a Cajun joke—a long story in Cajun dialect with a surprise ending. Then I would teach navigation, meteorology, aerodynamics, and aircraft instruments. Big John and I were in the same department; and besides teaching, we wrote and designed the programs of instruction. I was given the assignment to rearrange the entire program of instruction to match the correct phase of flight training. It was a real challenge and even more of a challenge to coordinate it implantation while phasing out the old program. John and I both made captain within a year and were then reassigned to our respective military branch schools.

I was given a direct commission into the air defense branch, so I was assigned to Fort Bliss in El Paso, Texas, for my basic branch course. The course provided the basics of the Army's arsenal of weapons to include nuclear warheads.

The Texas climate was totally opposite from Louisiana's. The first night in town I walked across the hotel lobby and touched the metal door; I thought I had been hit with a thousand volts of electricity! I had never experienced static electricity before that night. I had to be careful when I went to change my daughter's diaper at night: I had to touch something metal before I touched baby Allison or I would produce an arc of light in the dark, and one nervous baby!

Once I asked a question at the basic course which was never answered to my satisfaction. Based on the premise that the guidance system for the missile is dependent upon telemetry from radar, the first nuclear explosion would release so much RF (radioactive fallout/high radio frequency) energy into the atmosphere that all radar guidance would be lost and automatically would trigger the failsafe mechanism of any in-flight missiles and cause their self-destruction. Therefore, there could not be any true massive attack or counterattack once one nuclear bomb exploded. It left me with the impression that our defense system is only a deterrent and not really effective and is only good for a conventional war.

My next assignment was as range-control officer of the missile range near White Sands, New Mexico. We primarily fired Nike, Ajacks and Hawk missiles on 1200 acres of desert land. The only flying I could do was fly water buckets to distinguish range fires started by our missiles' impact. I enjoyed dove hunting with my commander, Colonel Eric Ericsson, out on the range. There was a lot of Indian history among the mesquite bushes and sand dunes. We would drive out on the weekends and hunt dove next to one of the few waterholes (called tanks in Texas) on our private range. The challenge was not shooting dove but how many you could hit with one shot.

I also applied my aviation knowledge to design and set up a gunship firing range to be used by the National Guard aviation units. But I felt somewhat of a half-ass, that is, half pilot and half field officer with no real future in the service. I did not have enough command time to allow me to progress in my branch; and because air defense had no need for an aviation unit, I had no future as an Army pilot.

I decided to leave the service and return to civilian life to complete a degree. I hoped to attend a veterinarian college. I flew for a medevac unit in the Louisiana National Guard for a year. Unfortunately, it was during fuel shortages and I was required to share the aircraft with another pilot. It was even harder to schedule an aircraft that I didn't redline due to mechanical problems. I found it harder and harder to get my flight hours in-between my busy college schedule, and the Guard just wasn't working out. I hated to leave the unit because I still loved to fly.

I had a 3.7 GPA at LSU and applied along with two hundred and fifty others for the thirty-two positions available at the new veterinarian college at LSU. When I was not accepted for the first enrollment class,

I had no choice except to leave college. To support my family I became a State Farm Insurance agent. Things always work out for the best: I love my job.

Today I would describe myself as being opinionated, but not political; persistent, but not a perfectionist; confident enough to be considered hardheaded. I am neither a hero nor a writer. I am an easy-going workaholic, a good storyteller, a potter, a part-time cook, and an early riser who does not depend on a clock or watch to know what time it is. I raise some birds, and enjoy fishing for bass with my son, Clint, or my long-time fishing buddy, David Thomas. It's a hard life!

MY DAUGHTER, WENDY

I also had a child with my first wife whom I divorced within a year of our daughter's birth. My ex-wife asked my consent for the adoption of our daughter by her new husband. After a lot of thought, I consented, realizing that the child could only be used as a weapon of revenge if I didn't. I had seen too much of that behavior by other split families and honestly felt it would be in the child's best interest. I also felt that the new husband, Jim, would be a good father and he was. When the adoption took place, I also honored their request not to interfere with their rearing of Wendy.

My parents meet Wendy after 17 years

I did manage to keep informed periodically about Wendy's life because my sister Suzie was married to the brother of my ex-wife's new husband. Got it? We all have a story to tell and I guess we all have some bad baggage; but like my daddy used to say, "Excuses are like assholes--everybody has one." Or was it noses? In any case, there are some things you can't go back and make right, but it's best to just move forward with your life and, hopefully, make fewer mistakes.

The good news is that my daughter, Wendy, and I met after twenty-seven years and we are now very close. When Wendy was 17, she asked her maternal grandmother, Laura, about her other grandparents and me. Laura was kind enough to arrange a meeting with my parents who were anxious to see Wendy. They all had a wonderful reunion; but unfortunately my ex-wife had a conniption (fit) when she found out, so everyone cooled it.

When I heard that Wendy had married Sean Rush who was in the Navy, I wrote to her. I felt released from the agreement of non-interference now that she was an adult. My first letter was to congratulate her on her recent marriage and to let her know that if she had any questions, I would try to respond as best I could. It was just letters between us for a long time, then pictures, and then we were on the phone regularly.

Wendy and Sean have two great kids: Jeremiah, who is sightless but plays the piano with perfect pitch, and Kaitlyn, who has an unusual talent for art and writing. Wendy home-schools and has provided a fine education to both of the grandkids. They used to live in San Diego, which our meeting until six years later, when they drove directly to New Orleans non-stop in a 1955 Chrysler New Yorker. It was a very warm and tender meeting for the first time since she was a baby.

It is great to be a part of Wendy's life again. Her husband was reassigned to a naval base in Corpus Christi, Texas, before he retired. Now Sean has left the Navy and has taken a position in Jacksonville, Florida performing the same kind of work Navy ships but now as a civilian contractor. We are family; Clint and Allison, are proud to have Wendy as a half-sister.

My daughter Allison has also recently moved to Destin, Florida with her husband, Christopher Blossman, to open up a new Parish National Bank branch for his family's business. Allison and Wendy are looking forward to getting together. Things do workout for the best in the long run.

My daughter Wendy Rush and her Family

CHAPTER 16

GOOD WARS VS. BAD WARS

I have never been a person who felt a need to join an association of any kind; but I did join the Vietnam Helicopter Pilot Association and later the Purple Heart Society. I used to be the president of our local chapter of VHPA. I just wanted to bring together pilots from the Louisiana and Mississippi area since there were a great number of pilots flying for oil companies in the Gulf region. But, like me, they were reluctant to join anything. It was hard to bring them all together on the same day for a crawfish boil because half of them were flying offshore and the others were off duty. Our local association fell apart due to the lack of interest.

The Purple Heart meetings were mostly soldiers from previous wars so I felt a little out of place. Plus the fact that I felt guilty that my injury was just a "John Wayne" scalp wound as compared to the more serious wounds these soldiers had received. The last meeting I attended around the D-Day anniversary was profound as I observed the veterans from the European campaign virtually fighting with the veterans from the Pacific campaign about who had had it the hardest. That would really be a hard question to answer. Both campaigns were hell since any particular day or beach assault could qualify as hell. Each soldier's perspective was a graded-level of hell. What is that magic threshold between not too nice and hell?

All wars deprive the soldiers of basic comforts, adequate sleep, and a general sense of well-being. Is it from witnessing the mass destruction of humans all around you? Probably, but if you survived as a witness, your experience would have only been a psychological hell. Hell on earth is defined as that which raises the "Pucker Factor" by the power of ten and increases exponentially by the numbers of hours exposed to such conditions.

Vietnam was a good war as far as wars go. We had air superiority, good equipment, great fire support, excellent medical response, and hot food--while the enemy had none of the above. All wars had their big battles such as Pork Chop Hill, Hamburger Hill, Bunker Hill, San Juan Hill, Gettysburg, Normandy, or Midway. All wars had their prisoner atrocities. All wars psychologically screwed up the survivors of that particular war to some degree. I am just glad I did not have to charge the cannon fire in the Civil War, or live in the muddy trenches of World War I, or fight house-to-house in the towns in France during World War II.

Wars like Korea and Vietnam were hard in the sense that they were without the total support of fellow Americans at home (in the good old U.S.A.). The other negative aspects of "my war" were booby traps, mines, and ambushes. But the good news was that we only had to go to Nam for one year, unlike past wars where you had to stay until the war was over or you were seriously wounded, or killed.

"My war" also had better medical evacuation than any prior war. A wounded soldier in the field could be in Japan within twenty-four hours. I even had a request on one medevac to bring a guy's leg so they could reattach it. Wounds were never as simple as pictured in war movies; most wounds had skin that was unattached to muscle, just flapping next to a gaping hole or lacerated limb. Our "MASH" units were not as primitive as the tent cities in Korea; even though some doctors used crazy glue to close wounds. It would stop the bleeding--allowing more time to treat the more serious injuries. Medevacs were in demand; pilots jumped at every opportunity to help out. I did an average of four a week, and that was not even my primary mission.

This war was not like wars of old where the survivors were the ones who had the physical ability and superior equipment to win. I would love to have gone sword-to-sword with Charlie. But the fact was that the little rice picker could fire his AK-47 from a thousand feet and take down Goliath. Actually, we all had a lot of respect for Charlie. We admired his tenacity under unbelievable conditions--with the most modern army in the world trying its best to blow him away.

To put things in perspective: we lose as many men, women, and children on our highways annually as we lost soldiers in the Vietnam War. Not to say that the loss of those men was not painful or in any way diminish their efforts and duty to our country. We all owe those who died and those who survived our complete debt of gratitude. But life and our freedom continue and that's why we went.

FORGIVENESS

One fact about past wars with civilized nations is that civil societies possess the capacity to forgive their enemy. It has been true throughout the history of man and especially our nation. It applies to the Indian War, Civil War, War for Independence, and both the World Wars. The vanquished have become allies. The healing power of the Civil War still amazes me. There is no hatred for the Indians, British, Japanese, or Germans. We joke about the Yankees down south and I am sure they joke about us, but we marry Yankees on a frequent basis. Assimilation by marriage always seems to heal animosities. There's some truth to the saying about lying down with your enemy.

The only civilizations that have problems with forgiveness are those nations that are politically founded in religious ideology. The scary problem with the Eastern nations like the Arab and the Far East (Asian) nations is their deep-seeded hatred that stems from millenniums of religious bias. After centuries of conquering, and slavery of the enemies' women, copulation among them has not had the same effect as it had with other nations because of their religious taboos--even though it is obvious that there was a lot of hanky-panky going on by all the conquerors.

Even Saddam Hussein, of questionable lineage anyway, may have had a long line of bastards and rapists in his family tree. Ironically, there is a strong probability that Saddam has quite a few Jewish genes within his screwed-up gene pool. Religious bias lies also with the people of India and Pakistan; and let us not excludes Ireland as another good example. Religion tends to separate rather than bind people of those nations. Religious tolerance would alleviate terrorism. There is some truth to the doctrine of separation of church and state.

CHAPTER 17

WHAT IT ALL MEANS

Now to address the question I proposed in my first chapter that applied to all of us who flew: "Why was I a survivor?" The best answer is "Why not?" By putting ourselves in harm's way, we automatically increased the probability of something unpleasant happening to us, and Charlie had his chance and blew it. We should focus on the good we accomplished and the nameless lives we saved. The courageous heroes we left behind paid the ultimate price for their devotion to duty as pilots: but we all consciously accepted that risk when we signed up for flight school.

Those who died had their moment in the sun, and they were as bright as the sun in that moment of death. It is our duty to tell their story and go on with our lives. Our duty now is to love our families and to help in the development of our kids and grandkids so that future generations will have the leadership and courage needed to live up to their potential.

There are two comments before closing: one is that I believe the draft would be a good thing with the proper exemptions applied. There is no reason why a young man should not devote a few years in the service of his country's defense to repay all those soldiers of past wars who defended the freedoms we enjoy today, especially while he is young and has not already established a career and family.

Service to your country gives direction to your life and can also make you an active participant in the future policies of America. There is no doubt that the Vietnam veteran has had more influence on the current leadership of our country than all the protesters of that war.

In the act of tough love, I forced my son, Clint, to join the service after a he had a disappointing freshman semester at college. Those were the last angry words we have ever had with each other. When I proposed military service to him, in outrage he said, "Okay, I will join the Marines tomorrow!" I commented, "Let's not get stupid!"

We sat down and discussed a logical approach to the situation and I even drove him over to Fort Rucker to take a flight physical to see if flying would be an option. Clint's eyes were in the early stages of myopia (nearsightedness) and the flight program was phased down to the point where the standards were high enough to disqualify him from entering the program. So we examined some other options and with his test-score level, he chose the Coast Guard and the opportunity to become an electrician--a decision that made his paternal grandfather very proud since that had also been his profession.

It was the proudest day in Clint's life and mine when I went to Cape May, New Jersey, for his graduation from boot camp. He went on to "A-school" (electrician school) in Yorktown, Virginia, and then reported to his final duty station in Mobile, Alabama. He left the service after two years and went back to college to graduate with A's and a degree in industrial technology. Not only did the military provide him with that self-confidence to take on any challenge, but it also gave him pride in the fact that he now felt he fulfilled his duty to his country.

Clint and I manage my office together which would normally require five sectaries for an agency my size. It is not only great having him work by with me; Clint is also indispensable to my operation. I sadly realize he must leave me someday to further his own career opening his own agency. I can only savor the moments until that day arrives.

To those of you who have a father, brother, or grandfather who served: encourage him to discuss his military experiences with you, or better yet, write or record his story. My paternal grandfather (the grumpy old fart) served with the "Rough Riders," yet he never spoke of his experiences. We have a portrait of his regimental company, but no one even knows for sure which man in the picture was Grandpa.

My last comment, but important to everyone who served: I understand your reluctance to share your experiences, but everyone has a story. Why not pass yours along to the next generation? Take pride in your heritage and your name. Think of all those names on a memorial wall that can't tell their story.

The Juge Tribe

Printed in the United States
19372LVS00001BB/121-522

9 781595 263155